SOMETHING MUST BE DONE
ABOUT MISS SEETON

The bathwater was hot, and Sir Sebastian Prothero soaked himself in it for a long time, going over and over every aspect of the situation, not wanting to face the fact that he was going to have to do something about Miss Seeton.

It was earlier, on the way to Canterbury, that the possibility of murdering her had occurred to him, to be dismissed at once as being out of the question. He was a master criminal, certainly, but no murderer. But the insidious thought kept coming back, in subtly different ways. Not a killer? The former Captain Prothero of the Guards was, like most professional soldiers, a *trained* killer. And we all have to die sometime. Miss Seeton was elderly. Not all that many years to go in any case. Above all, she was dangerous.

He hauled himself up out of the water and reached for the bath towel. It would have to be done that night.

Heron Carvic's Miss Seeton

MISS SEETON, BY APPOINTMENT

HAMPTON CHARLES

BERKLEY BOOKS, NEW YORK

MISS SEETON, BY APPOINTMENT

A Berkley Book/published by arrangement with
the author and the Estate of Heron Carvic

PRINTING HISTORY
Berkley edition/April 1990

ISBN: 0-425-12100-3

A BERKLEY BOOK® TM 757,375
Berkley Books are published by The Berkley Publishing Group,
200 Madison Avenue, New York, New York 10016.
The name "BERKLEY" and the "B" logo
are trademarks belonging to Berkley Publishing Corporation.

PRINTED IN THE UNITED STATES OF AMERICA

10 9 8 7 6 5 4

For Anthea Morton-Saner,
who makes the improbable come to pass

chapter
~1~

"MORNIN', GORGEOUS," said Bert the postman, taking his time over looking through his bundle of mail. He was a perky young man with a shock of red hair, an émigré cockney who enjoyed life in Kent, especially in the summer. And more particularly still, he enjoyed the one week in three when he was on the Plummergen round. For most Plummergen residents the sight of the little red post office van was the high point of the day, and they nearly all came to their doors for their letters and a bit of a chat. The Nuts, as they were known in the village, and whom Bert had privately christened The Long and Short of It, never failed. The rotund Mrs. Norah Blaine was usually civil enough in a fussy sort of way, but it made Bert's day when Miss Erica Nuttel got there first, for with her he was engaged in an unceasing and to him highly enjoyable battle of wits.

"'Ardly your lucky day, ducks." He doled out the items one by one, with a running commentary. "Gas bill. Picture postcard of Wookey 'Ole, where Maureen's 'avin' a super time, bless 'er cotton socks. *Psychic News* in a plain wrapper an' I should think so, too. Load o' codswallop if you want my opinion—"

"I don't," Erica Nuttel snapped. "And moreover I take the greatest possible exception both to your impertinent familiarity and your reading a personal message addressed to me. The district postmaster will most certainly hear about this."

Bert grinned, unabashed. "Cor! 'Ark 'oo's talkin'! Know what your trouble is, donecher? Jealous. Tell you what, give us a kiss and I'll let you 'ave a look through the rest. Some good stuff 'ere. Take Sir George up at Rytham 'All. 'Is nibs an' 'er Ladyship keep up a very good class o' correspondence, 'n' they ain't the only ones. Some o' your neighbors get 'oliday postcards from places an 'ell of a lot more exotic than Wookey bleedin' 'Ole, I can tell yer. An' they 'ave some 'ighly exclusive pen pals, too. F'rinstance, guess 'oo's got a letter from the Queen, then?"

He plucked a large, opulent-looking envelope from the bundle and brandished its reverse so that Miss Nuttel could see the gold coat of arms embossed on the flap. "Sockin' great typewriter she must 'ave there at Buck 'Ouse. Comes out like them large print books I get my mum down Brettenden Li'bry. She likes anything a bit saucy, Mum does. O ho! 'Oity toity! Like that, is it?" Bert added to the door, which had been slammed in his face. "An' up yours, too!"

He put his tongue out, made an exceedingly vulgar gesture with his free hand in the full awareness that one or both of The Nuts would be observing him from behind the net curtains, and crossed the road to the garage. His van was already parked outside Mr. Stillwell's hardware and general store, inside which lurked the little counter that constituted Plummergen's sub-post office. This would be Bert's last port of call in the village proper, when he emptied the pillar-box and went in to pick up registered mail and parcels to take back to base with him. Plummergen being a compact sort of village, it was convenient to leave the van there and make deliveries on foot, popping back to it for another bundle as necessary.

"Oh, Eric, you are mean! *Do* let me have a go with the binoculars!" Norah Blaine positively quivered with impatience, but Miss Nuttel continued her vigil from her perch on the chair she had placed by one of the upstairs windows facing the street, adjusting the focus from time to time to keep Bert under scrutiny as he continued on his jauntily eccentric way up The Street.

"Be quiet, Bunny. And stop plucking at my slacks; I'm trying to concentrate. You know you can never focus binoculars properly, anyway. He did it quite deliberately, you know. He's been back to the van twice already, each time with just that one big envelope in his hand. Making sure everybody in the village knows about it."

"Well, it *is* interesting, after all," Norah expostulated. "If it had been me, I'd have grabbed it from him and had a good look at the address for myself."

Miss Nuttel sniffed. "Don't be ridiculous; you'd have done nothing of the kind. You let that ghastly young man with his crude innuendos intimidate you. Besides, it's obvious it must be for the Colvedens. Sir George is a justice of the peace, after all. The letter is undoubtedly from the palace. Perhaps he's going to be made lord lieutenant of the county."

"Or a deputy lieutenant," suggested Norah, who was inclined to be less bold in her speculations. "Is there just one of those, by the way, or are there several?"

"I really couldn't say. And frankly, Bunny, the question is academic so far as we're concerned. If you really want to know, you could always ring up the *Daily Telegraph* . . . Oh, *no*! It's *too much*!"

Mrs. Blaine did her fluffy best to bristle. "Well, really, Eric! I was only *asking* . . ."

Erica Nuttel scrambled down, an expression of outrage on her face. "He's delivered it to *that woman*!"

It took a few seconds for Norah Blaine's ineffectual protests to die down and for her friend's news to sink in. Even then she opened and closed her little goldfish mouth several times before she was able to regain the power of speech. "Miss *Seeton*?" she quavered at last. "A letter from Buckingham Palace?"

"For *me*? From Buckingham Palace? Oh, dear, surely not! How very extraordinary! There must be some mistake . . ."

"Nah, no mistake, Miss S.," Bert said, beaming at Miss Emily Seeton reassuringly. "Cheer up; if the beefeaters lock you up in the Tahra London, me an' me mates'll 'ave you out in no time." He winked conspiratorially at Martha Bloomer, who had bustled into view behind her, bearing a dust pan and brush. Martha, who lived practically next door to Sweetbriars and "did" for Miss Seeton as necessary, had a rosy, generous soul. Moreover, she hailed originally from London, her Plummergen-born husband, Stan, having wooed and won her during a hop-picking season long ago, when Londoners by the hundreds—including Martha and her family—used to flock from the East End to earn a few pounds as casual helpers. The passage of the years had changed her in many ways, but she still remembered a thing or two about the way to deal with cockney sauce.

"The Tower? My goodness, I certainly hope not . . ." Miss Seeton was saying distractedly as Martha unceremoniously relieved her of the imposing missive and studied it briefly.

"Now, you pay no mind to his nonsense," she said decisively. "He's just trying to tease you, miss. There's a card in there; I can feel it. Miss Emily D. Seeton, Sweetbriars, Plummergen, Kent. That's an invite, that is, plain as a pikestaff."

"No flies on you, Mrs. B., is there? She's dead right." Bert adopted a ludicrously fluting falsetto as he pretended to usher Miss Seeton to a table. "*Soo* glad you could join us in partakin' of this 'ere collation, Miss Seeton. Do just kaindly sit 'ere between Lord Muck and the Dook of Owsyourfather. Oh, and maind the old dook don't slosh 'is soup all over yer frock, love."

"Give over, Bert."

Sensing that Mrs. Bloomer was beginning to hoist storm cones, Bert reverted to his normal manner. "Yeah, right. Sorry, Miss S., jus' my little joke. What I reckon is, it's for one o' them garden parties. An' you'll 'ave some company, 'cos I got another one just like it in my bag, for Sir George 'n' 'is lady. Go on, open it; it won't bite."

Not wholly convinced that it wouldn't, Miss Seeton would have preferred to retreat to the privacy of her bedroom and run through a few of her yoga exercises before opening the royal missive. At the same time she realized that such a course of action would constitute cruel and unnatural punishment for both faithful Mrs. Bloomer and for cheery Bert, of whom she had become quite fond since coming to live in Plummergen. "Yes, well, perhaps, but it would never do to tear the flap, would it—oh, is that a penknife? How thoughtful...*well*, you're both right! Fancy! It says 'I am commanded by Her Majesty to request the pleasure of the company of Miss Emily Seeton at a Garden Party to be given...' Me! Invited to a royal garden party!" Of course, I couldn't possibly go—"

"Wotcher mean, not go?"

"Not *go*? Whyever not?"

Faced with a united front of indignant astonishment on

the part of her two friends, Miss Seeton frankly dithered. It was a great relief to her when Bert eventually decided that duty called him elsewhere, and took himself off vowing to return to the charge the following morning after discussing the matter with his mum. Then Martha Bloomer very sensibly prescribed a cup of tea and one of the ginger chocolate biscuits Mrs. Stillwell had begun to stock a few months earlier, and within half an hour at least some of Miss Seeton's perturbation had subsided.

By the time she had finished her modest lunch she was feeling timidly elated, and was even toying with the idea of accepting the invitation, with which a printed reply card had been thoughtfully enclosed. If Sir George and Lady Colveden had indeed received a similar invitation, it made a great difference, of course, but Bert might have been teasing about that, too. As well as about the Tower of London, that is. Such a good-humored young man; much too young to know that nobody had been locked up in the Tower since the unfortunate Sir Roger Casement, so strange for a family to be named after a kind of window. On the other hand there was a herald called Portcullis—a pretty name but not perhaps as nice as Bluemantle Pursuivant—and thinking of gates and apertures of one sort and another, what about Lord Portal who had been something important to do with the air force—or was that Lord Trench, no, Trench*ard*, surely?

Miss Seeton had moved on in her reverie through Trenchard—who confusingly made her think of policemen as well as airmen—to trench coats, riding breeches, breeches buoys, and Grace Darling when the sound of somebody tapping at the window dragged her to the surface of her stream of consciousness, and she looked up to see Nigel Colveden outside. At once she gave him a little wave, and hastened to the front door to let him in.

"My dear Nigel, how very nice to see you! I'd quite

forgotten you must be on vacation by now, and what lovely weather you have brought with you! Come in, come in. Have you had lunch? Mrs. Bloomer went home a long time ago, but if you're hungry, I'm sure I could make you a sandwich—"

"Thanks all the same, Miss Seeton, but I had lunch a couple of hours ago. It is ten past three, you know."

"Good gracious, is it really? I'm afraid I've been daydreaming again. About Lord Portal, and shipwrecks came into it, too, for some odd reason. Well, a cup of tea, perhaps, while you tell me all your news."

Sir George and Lady Colveden's son and heir was twenty, and a student at an agricultural college. No intellectual giant, he was nevertheless a pleasant, open, and on occasion resourceful young man who had more than once appointed himself Miss Seeton's protector and rendered her sterling service. His principal interests in life were his MG sports car and whichever young woman he was currently infatuated with.

Miss Seeton had been acquainted with the Colvedens for no more than two or three years, but could remember several of Nigel's inamoratas, who were almost invariably as unsuitable as they were glamorous. The gleam in his eye told her the situation was normal: namely, that Nigel Colveden had a new girlfriend, but naturally one could hardly ask him outright. That would never do.

"Well, Nigel, tell me about your new girlfriend," she heard herself suggesting as she offered him one of the really quite excellent biscuits, and sat down rather suddenly, warm with embarrassment.

"Oh, Lord, does it show that much?" Nigel's grin indicated that he was both unabashed and more than ready to launch into a lyrical account of his latest entanglement. Reassured, Miss Seeton sipped her own tea and waited.

"Yes. Well, wow! You'd never guess in a million years,

but I've met Marigold Naseby. *The* Marigold Naseby!"

"Er . . . how very nice, Nigel. Do forgive me, but I'm not absolutely sure—"

"You *must* know, Miss Seeton, it's been in the papers! The Lalique Lady."

"Lalique? Oh, such a wonderfully *bold* vision for a jeweler, but then did he not create pieces for Sarah Bernhardt? One does so regret having been born too late to see her perform . . . perhaps even wearing a Lalique piece. You *are* referring to the great Lalique?"

"Yes, yes, at least I suppose so, but the important thing is that Marigold Naseby has been chosen as the Lalique Lady! Following The Search of the Century for Cedric's Symbol. Cedric *Benbow.*"

Miss Seeton began to feel just a little less mystified by Nigel's sudden expression of interest in Lalique. She had given up reading newspapers years before, finding them increasingly depressing, and generally turned the radio off after the weather forecast. She was nevertheless not wholly without access to news. Martha Bloomer, for instance, liked to discuss lunar exploration and the like, having a cousin by marriage who claimed to have seen a flying saucer in the night sky over Tenterden.

Moreover, Miss Seeton occasionally took tea with the vicar and his sister, and the Reverend Arthur Treeves from time to time ventured an opinion about events in the world outside Plummergen. Whenever this happened the formidable Miss Molly Treeves corrected him on the facts and challenged his interpretation of them, and Miss Seeton was inclined to let it all wash over her. She was, however, perfectly sure that she would have taken note if either of the Treeveses had mentioned the name of Cedric Benbow.

"Miss Naseby is a friend of Cedric Benbow? Well, I never! Do you know, Nigel, that I was at art school with Cedric Benbow? Such a strange boy he was then, much troubled by acne, and, dare I say it, with a rather common way of speaking. None of us imagined for a second that he would go on to such great things."

Nigel regarded Miss Seeton with something approaching awe. It had become clear even to him that, astonishingly enough, she had never heard of Marigold Naseby. On the other hand she was claiming acquaintance with the legendary Cedric Benbow, the gilded young dilettante of the thirties who had become Mayfair's leading portrait photographer and dabbled in theatrical design before achieving worldwide fame as the grand old man of fashion photography.

"Gosh," he said reverently.

chapter

-2-

"HANG ON a minute, Chris. I'll just jot these names down."
While he reached for his scratch pad Chief Superintendent
Delphick tried cradling the telephone receiver to his ear
with his shoulder in the way people in films seemed to
manage so deftly, and as always it fell with a clatter to his
desk. As he picked it up again he darted a stern look across
the room in the direction of Detective Sergeant Bob
Ranger, but he was too late: his gentle giant of an assistant
had already spun round in his chair and was rummaging in
the small filing cabinet beside his desk while suppressing a
grin. After putting Chief Inspector Brinton of the Kent police through to The Oracle, he'd made a private bet with
himself that the conversation between the two old friends
would be a lengthy one and that The Oracle would drop the
phone at least once. Brainy he undoubtedly was, but Bob
would hate to see his boss in charge of a chain saw.

"Sorry about that. The Colvedens I know quite well, of
course, including young Nigel. And I've heard of Cedric
Benbow; who hasn't? But who's Lalik? Sounds like one of

those fishy Lebanese wheeler-dealers with a flat in Eaton Square and a finger in too many pies for his own good. What? Oh, I see. L-A-L-I-Q-U-E. Famous jeweler. Yes, yes, now I'm with you. I should have twigged when you mentioned Benbow. There's been something in the *Daily Negative* about it, I recall. What do you mean, a rag?" A pause to give the idea brief consideration. "Well, I suppose it is, really. But having had dealings with the lady, I enjoy reading Amelita Forby's pieces. So this Marigold Naseby's the girl who won the competition, is she? Tell me more."

Delphick listened attentively for some time, a slow smile spreading over his face, and made a few more notes before he spoke again. "Take your point, Chris. I can't see Miss Seeton making the front page of *Mode* magazine either, but then again no rational person could have envisaged her getting involved with those devil-worshippers of yours. Apart from the fact that she lives in Plummergen and knows the Colvedens, she has nothing whatever to do with this project, you say. And neither do you and your merry men . . . officially, anyway. Ah, well, forewarned is forearmed, I suppose. Your sinking feeling is entirely understandable, though. No, nice try, but I haven't anything to occupy her with somewhere else for a few days. Do give me a ring when it's all over. Hope it keeps fine for you."

After putting the phone down Delphick pondered for a minute or two, then turned to Ranger. "Been down to Plummergen to see your intended lately, Bob?"

"Most weekends when I can get away, sir."

"Run into Miss Seeton recently?"

"Anne and I met her in the street just last Sunday, as a matter of fact. She'd been to church. We chatted for a few minutes." Bob looked embarrassed. "Sorry, sir, I forgot to tell you she sent her regards."

"How kind. While Chief Inspector Brinton's sitting there in Ashford having kittens about her. Had you any idea that Rytham Hall boasts a couple of the finest William Morris rooms in England?"

"Can't say I had." Bob Ranger had learned to live with The Oracle's habit of changing the subject without warning.

"Well, we both know now, don't we? It seems that *Vogue* or some similar glossy magazine—no, actually it was *Mode* he mentioned—is preparing a very elaborate feature involving some fancy new collection of clothes. They've hired old Benbow at vast expense to do the photography and he's turning the whole thing into a terrific production, to be shot inside and outside Rytham Hall. By kind permission of Sir George and Lady Colveden, and no doubt by special arrangement with money."

"Sorry to be dim, sir, but why should that bother Mr. Brinton?"

"Several reasons. Item: a collection of Lalique jewelry said to be worth millions is being put together with the collaboration of museums in Lisbon and Paris, and brought over on loan to make the frocks look even posher. One of the most reputable private security companies in the country has been hired to keep an eye on these baubles, but Sir George thought there'd be no harm in giving the chief constable a ring to put him in the picture." Delphick paused, scratched his head, and gazed thoughtfully at the ceiling before going on.

"Item: at Benbow's instigation what amounts to a national beauty contest was staged to find a model with what he deemed to be the right face—and figure, presumably— to go with the clothes and the Lalique trinkets. The lucky girl is the hitherto unknown Marigold Naseby, now famous to readers of the tabloid press even though she hasn't done anything yet, and destined—for a few months until the next Face of the Century appears on the scene—to command astronomical fees. Thus, it seems an enormous

amount of publicity has been generated. The fact that
Rytham Hall is to be the setting for Benbow's pics has not
been announced, but following his chat with Sir George it
has occurred to Mr. Brinton's chief constable that anybody
who has the least interest in finding out could do so easily.
It has further struck him that the better class of jewel thief
might see the project as a challenge."

"I can see how he might, sir."

"Great minds indeed think alike. So although responsibility for safekeeping of the goodies rests with the Securicor people or whomever, I'm sure you'll understand why
the CC's meditations have given Mr. Brinton pause for
thought, too. And why Mr. Brinton's unease is heightened
by the fact that all this hoopla is due to be staged in the
near future within easy walking distance of Miss Emily D.
Seeton's modest residence."

"He's afraid she'll get involved somehow."

"You catch on fast, Bob." Delphick's smile de-barbed
the remark. "He's not only afraid she will; he's jolly sure
she will. And who are we to make light of his premoni-
tions?"

Miss Seeton was simultaneously the subject of conversation in another larger and more opulently furnished office
in Scotland Yard: that occupied by Sir Hubert Everleigh,
the assistant commissioner (Crime). With him was dapper
Roland Fenn, deputy assistant commissioner in charge of
Special Branch, with whom Sir Hubert was sporadically at
war and was currently arguing, but on this occasion comparatively mildly. "I still can't for the life of me imagine
why you're so insistent on keeping Delphick in the dark
over this. If Miss Seeton has a line manager in this place,
he's it."

Fenn laid a finger alongside his nose. "The need to
know, Hubert, the need to know. I keep pointing this out to

you. Besides, it's absurd to use the expression 'line manager' in connection with Miss Seeton. She gets an annual retainer as an occasional, what, consultant, I suppose."

"Artist. That's what she thinks her job is, and that's how she should be referred to."

"All right, then, artist. And admittedly Delphick more or less recruited her."

"He did indeed. And I might point out that you more than once expressed the view that he was off his head, until you found out for yourself how useful she can be."

"Granted. But nevertheless, she's not a member of Delphick's staff, and I repeat, he doesn't know. That's the whole point. And come to think of it, I'm not altogether convinced *you* need to know."

Sir Hubert bristled. "Now look here, I'm well aware that you Special Branch fellows seem to think you can do as you like and go about hugging secrets to your bosoms, but remember who pays your salary, *Mister Fenn*. And bear in mind that there are a few of us in this building who happen to be senior to you. And have at least as many well-placed cronies in the Home Office as you do."

The AC knew it was not in Fenn's nature to apologize, but the way the younger man was scrutinizing his beautifully manicured fingernails suggested a certain discomfiture, so he harrumphed briefly and then adopted a more friendly manner. "Right, yes. Must get on. She's accepted the invitation, then. Good."

"Yes. Practically everybody who gets one does, of course; thrilled to bits, but I was glad when I heard. On the other hand one mustn't expect too much of the good lady. One of my chaps can easily enough steer her in Wormelow Tump's direction and get a conversation going. Even, with a bit of luck, contrive some sort of an incident to ensure that Tump makes more of an impression on her than the other strangers she'll meet. But it's a bit much to hope he'll trigger off one of her extraordinary psychological insights in the space of a few minutes at most."

Sir Hubert nodded soberly enough. "Yes. And on reflection I realize you're right that she mustn't be told a thing, not even that we want to know what she makes of his state of mind." He sighed. "Your friends in Curzon Street do seem to make things unnecessarily complicated, I must say. If MI5 have their doubts about this fellow's loyalties *and* think somebody might be putting the squeeze on him, why not do the obvious thing and have a quiet word with him themselves? Get him to resign. Once he does that, no problem, eh?"

Fenn closed his eyes briefly and put on the long-suffering expression he was so good at. Then, remembering how close he had come to outright insubordination a little earlier, he cleared his throat and relied on blandness instead, throwing in a rare "sir" for good measure.

"Let me try to make myself clearer, sir. As you know, I have regular liaison meetings with senior staff at MI5, and this problem has been aired several times over the past few months. There's one chap there—better be nameless, I suppose, but he's a great one for seeing Reds under every bed. Has a bee in his bonnet about Harold Wilson, too. Funny chap all round, actually; talks about retiring to Tanzania, or is it Tasmania?"

"What the devil does it matter where the blighter retires to? Do get on."

"Sorry. Well, he's convinced that friend Tump was got at before the war when he was up at Cambridge, like all those others, and that he's been beavering away for the other side ever since."

"Yes, yes, I've heard all that before. But doing what, for goodness sake? Telling the Russians there's woodworm in the coronation chair? Bugging Her Majesty's Fabergé paperweight? Damn it all, the fellow's only some sort of

glorified warehouseman at Buck House, isn't he? Takes
care of all the useless loot that gets showered on the royals
everywhere they go, as I understand it. Ceremonial elephant's foot umbrella holders, models of the Taj Mahal
made of spent matches, that kind of thing. Pity it can't all
go straight to Oxfam, in my opinion."

"Forgive me for saying so, but it's not quite like that,
Sir Hubert. You mentioned a Fabergé paperweight yourself, and for all we know HM may very well use one. The
Royal Collection of Objets de Vertu is literally priceless,
although I agree it probably does include some pretty odd
bits and pieces. As its custodian, Sir Wormelow Tump is a
senior courtier in frequent personal contact with members
of the royal family. He is also one of the greatest living
experts on lacquer, or enamel or something. Imagine how
embarrassing it would be if he were to be exposed as, well,
not perhaps exactly as a traitor, because I'm sure you're
right in thinking it's unlikely he could ever have been of
any political use to the other side. But splashed all over the
papers as the Queen's spy-in-waiting! The headline writers
would have a field day."

"That's precisely the point I've been laboring, my dear
man! They should simply get rid of the chap right away.
Damage limitation. Might still cause a bit of a hoo-hah if
he gets found out later on, but not nearly so bad as if he's
still in the job."

"Quite so, but only if this particular MI5 man's right.
He's persuaded one or two other senior people to take his
part, but there are others equally sure it's a lot of nonsense.
Heads would most certainly roll if Tump let it be known he
was being pressurized to resign and was refusing because
he's innocent. Even interrogating him might upset the ap-
plecart. He's on the touchy side, I gather."

"So MI5 can't agree on whether to let sleeping dogs lie
or feel his collar, and you volunteered Miss Seeton to pro-

vide a diagnosis and make up their minds for them."

The Special Branch man had the grace to color slightly. "It does sound ridiculous put like that, but, yes, in a way, except that I haven't told them. And don't intend to, unless by some miracle she comes up with something brilliant. What happened is that I was asked if I'd picked up any gossip about Tump from the branch men we have in place in the palace all the time. So I had a discreet word with several of them myself. Most of them have never met him. Among those that have, the general view seems to be that at worst he's inclined to be snooty. Nothing of any possible use to MI5 emerged. Ultimately the director of MI5 will have to decide what to do, no doubt after having a word with the PM. Miss Seeton might just conceivably help to resolve the squabbling at Curzon Street, though. And even if she doesn't, well, she'll have enjoyed her tea and cake in the palace grounds and be none the wiser."

"If I know our Miss S., she'll be none the wiser whatever happens. That woman's a human lightning conductor: the bit that's left standing when everything else in sight has collapsed. Well, let's hope she turns up trumps for you. I'm bound to say that inserting Miss Seeton deliberately into any situation always seems to produce results, if not necessarily the ones intended."

"May I be assured, then, that you won't mention any of this to Delphick . . . sir?"

"Oh, very well. Not beforehand, anyway. You must jolly well keep me posted, though. Agreed?"

"Naturally. Perhaps you'd excuse me now."

Sir Hubert nodded and Fenn got up to go. As he reached the door the assistant commissioner voiced an afterthought. "Satisfy my curiosity over one small matter, would you? How did you organize the invitation?"

Fenn smiled his private smile. "Simplicity itself. We're shown the invitation lists for these occasions as a matter of routine, and this isn't the first time we've suggested one or two additions. Why, would you and Lady Everleigh like to go sometime?"

Sir Hubert's response was straight from the deep freeze. "Thank you for the suggestion, Mr. Fenn, but my wife and I do not require your assistance. We have been privileged to be Her Majesty's guests before. On a number of occasions. And don't push your luck, laddie."

chapter
~3~

SIR SEBASTIAN Prothero took a shortcut through Carnaby Street, glancing now and then with tolerant amusement at a youngster in particularly absurd clothes. He actually stopped short to study one young man whose flowing locks were secured by a headband and who was wearing tight pink plush trousers that flared out further down, a fringed sash that looked suspiciously like an old tablecloth, and a brocade waistcoat but no shirt. Prothero's amusement was, however, soon tinged with regrets evoked by the realization that at thirty-seven he was probably old enough to be the father of most of the people around him. Indeed, on further reflection it occurred to him it was perfectly possible he *was* the father of one or two of them; that among these teenagers in their union jack underwear and maxi-skirts there might be a bearer of the Prothero genes. He shuddered delicately, and turned his mind to other, much less depressing concerns.

In fact, it was he who cut the oddest figure in Carnaby Street that morning, being turned out in a style much more appropriate to Pall Mall, half a mile to the southeast. He was wearing a Gieves and Hawkes suit, whose makers had also supplied his socks. His gleaming shoes were by Lobb of St. James's, and the made-to-measure shirt setting off the tie of his former Guards regiment so beautifully had come from Turnbull and Asser. Sir Sebastian had a perfect right to wear the tie. He had not, after all, been cashiered following that unfortunate sequence of events seven or eight years earlier; it had merely been suggested—strongly suggested—that he would be wise to resign his commission.

At the time he had felt distinctly hard done by. After all, it was hardly his fault that the adjutant's seventeen-year-old daughter Fiona had fallen for him, had a glass or two of champagne too many at the regimental ball, and made that silly exhibition of herself; just rotten luck that the child knew perfectly well Sebastian was having an enjoyable affair with her mother at the time and passed on the information to the great number of people within fascinated earshot during the time it took the purple-faced adjutant to hustle her off the premises.

Anybody involved in a distracting situation like that could be forgiven for getting his cash-flow arrangements in a bit of a muddle, surely? It was only a few checks that subsequently bounced: but from the way Colonel Henry had gone on during that memorable half hour you'd have thought he'd tried to blow up the Bank of England. Prothero still thought it very stuffy on Henry's part to have insisted that he should go, but did take his point that the adjutant was an excellent marksman who might well be looking forward to the next time the battalion went out on a field training exercise.

In the event everything had turned out for the best. His own father, the fifth baronet, had died a few months later after falling off his horse while riding with the North

Herefordshire hunt near Bromyard, and that had helped a lot. The old boy left a fair few debts of his own, but what might well have been a bleak outlook for a disgraced ex-Captain Prothero looked very different to the newly-styled Sir Sebastian.

One or two none-too-scrupulous entrepreneurs were alert to the advantages from a PR point of view of putting the name of a titled "director" on their letterheads and were prepared to pay a couple of thousand a year for the privilege. Then the Mondial Club acquired a gambling license and opened its leather-padded doors to well-heeled gamblers, and Prothero made the acquaintance of Reg Cobb, who was its real owner but shunned the limelight. Reg sized the presentable young baronet up in no time and soon offered him drinks and dinners on the house in return for his mere presence there for a few hours three or four evenings a week.

For Reg frequently described himself, a trifle floridly and with an engaging disregard for the mixed metaphor, as a rough diamond who had been schooled in the great university of life. In order to obtain the club's gambling license he had persuaded a few respectable and mostly decrepit old buffers to join the board of directors, but was well aware that he needed a first-rate front man. Within a matter of weeks he recognized that Sir Sebastian Prothero was that man. Prothero had no doubts either, then or later.

Handsome, suave, and exquisitely turned out, he was witty and affable with the male clientele, charming and courteous with the ladies. He had learned the hard way the importance of discretion, and when one or two of the latter indicated they might not be averse to getting to know him better, he followed up their hints with increasingly elegant savoir faire. The platinum cuff links from Asprey's which he was wearing that day were an early gift from a grateful American lady, and for the slender Patek Philippe watch on his wrist he was indebted to the no-longer-bored wife of a racehorse owner who was seldom at home.

Thanks largely to Prothero—as Reg Cobb was smart enough to acknowledge—the Club Mondial rapidly became much more than a resort for wealthy gamblers: it turned into a nightclub—*the* place to be seen, and consequently a happy hunting ground for gossip writers. Prothero accepted the substantial salary Reg Cobb now paid him as no more than his due, but it suited him to cultivate his image as a cross between a gigolo and a PR man long after he had acquired a taste for more exacting and interesting activities.

The traumatic experience of being booted out of the Guards was the making of Sir Sebastian Prothero. He discovered in himself hitherto unsuspected intellectual resources, and the capacity for detached thought. Ensconced in the Club Mondial, he realized that while he could reasonably hope to continue to make a comfortable living from his looks and style until he was well into his forties, the time would inevitably come when this option would no longer be open to him. It was therefore advisable to consider possible alternatives.

Marriage was one. There were plenty of women about who would fall over themselves for the chance to become Lady Prothero, needless to say. The snag was that the rich ones were usually in that happy state because they had rich husbands, and would cease to be so were they to divorce. And the unmarried ones were largely on the make, like himself. Prothero wouldn't have minded taking on a daughter of the aristocracy, but unfortunately people in those circles had long memories and knew too much about his past to find him acceptable. He lost no sleep over this: marriage would cramp his style anyway, and hamper his other, confidential career: a career embarked on more or less accidentally but which was now shaping up splendidly.

It had all started when one of the gossip writers who had begun to frequent the club put it bluntly to Prothero that he was in a position to pay good money for whatever newsworthy tidbits of scandal he might be disposed to pass on. "Your own anonymity absolutely guaranteed, dear boy. We journalists have our code, you know. Protect our sources. Only interested in exclusives, needless to say. Cutthroat business, this is." Prothero had already come to the conclusion that most of the people he met were stupider than he was, and charitably pointed out that if the hack wanted to work out who was sleeping with whom he had only to use his eyes and ears and a bit of imagination for half an hour on any given evening at the club.

"Take your point, old boy, but you're here practically all the time, right? And people sort of treat you as part of the furniture—no offense, but you know what I mean. Bet they come out with all manner of goodies in front of you when they've had a few. Apart from that, a photocopy of your membership list would be worth a bob or two to me. Especially if annotated with your comments." The slimy little man had been right, of course, but what he hadn't expected was that, having eventually established precisely how much he meant by "a bob or two," Prothero would turn him down with a great show of outraged probity.

The hapless journalist had been right in emphasizing that gossip writing was a cutthroat business. Prothero tipped off one of his tempter's more sophisticated rivals on another paper, who was happy to pay half as much again as the proffered "bob or two" for the means to discredit part of the opposition. This highly successful deal marked the beginning of a relationship that greatly profited both parties. Prothero was indeed in a position to pass on intriguing nuggets of information to his new friend, who thereby achieved a number of what passed for as scoops in his tawdry world.

Inspired by the success of the arrangement, Prothero set up an independent and just as confidential deal with a notorious candid cameraman. This paparazzo specialized in surprising the famous and the glamorous in circumstances they had fondly imagined to be private; and Prothero was often able to tip him off when there was money to be made. The intrepid lensman hawked the less explicit photographs round the British tabloids. Some of the more outré ones found a good home on the Continent, in the pages of the kind of magazines that were forever announcing the Queen's impending divorce; and Prothero rather fancied that the real sizzlers were usually purchased for substantial sums by or on behalf of their subjects.

In short, Sir Sebastian had, as we have seen, become a realist. As such, he was well aware on that July day in Carnaby Street that he was not only a purveyor of gossip and scandal but also its subject in some quarters. He surmised, correctly, that his name was well-known to certain police officers based at West End Central headquarters whose job it was to keep a discreet eye on such establishments as the Club Mondial. He liked to think that they probably had him down as a contemptible but essentially petty crook, a smoothie con man who sponged off rich women and easy marks, a parasite happily pocketing kickbacks from his Fleet Street cronies. He was content that this should be so. It made it much less likely that they would for a moment connect him with the succession of daring jewel robberies that were greatly exercising a number of provincial police forces, not to mention certain insurance companies.

For Sir Sebastian Prothero was, in his own estimation at least, a criminal mastermind, well on the way that day to perfecting plans for what he confidently intended to be his most audacious coup to date.

• • •

A mile or so to the east in Fleet Street, Mel Forby was choosing her words with more care than she generally did when arguing with the editor of the *Daily Negative*. The editor for his part was still trying to come to terms with the young woman who had when he first knew her worn intimidating eye makeup and affected an extraordinary and completely bogus American accent, using a vocabulary derived, he thought, from old B movies and hard-boiled private-eye stories. Mel had never actually rushed into his office shouting "Hold the front page!" but he had lived in daily expectation of it. Until, that is, something had transformed her. Her eyes now looked as lustrous as her hair was soft and her figure was voluptuous, while her manner of speech was straightforward, warmed by the hint of the Liverpool accent she had previously tried so hard to varnish over.

At first he, like practically everybody else in the office, assumed she must be in love. The problem with that theory was that Mel showed no sign of floating through life in a romantic haze. On the contrary, she was as tough, intelligent, and resourceful as ever, and her new image and manner made her more formidable, not less. For the people she dealt with were disarmed and bemused by her, and only afterward—sometimes—realized they had been up against an expert.

"I still don't get it," the editor said plaintively. "Okay, so you started off with us covering the rag trade, and nobody's saying you didn't do a great job. But now you're a reporter with a well-known byline. You get paid a lot more; you can write about pretty well what you like, especially crime. Except that, well, look at it this way: Pete Morgan would blow a fuse if you suggested covering the Cup Final instead of him. Jason Lombard would have a fit if you were to make a takeover bid for his financial pages. So it's hardly surprising that Sue's up in arms over you hijacking this Cedric Benbow nonsense. Sue's your *successor*, remember? She writes about fashion now. And while we're at it, I may say I'm not all that thrilled about the way you've been giving all this free publicity to *Mode* in your pieces lately. I know it's hardly a competitor, but have you got shares in it or something?"

Mel hoped very much that she wasn't visibly blushing. "Of course I haven't. I'm sorry Sue's upset, and I wish she'd spoken to me about it. I'm sure I could have made her see that this is really art we're talking about, not fashion. And the *Negative* doesn't run to an art correspondent. Anyway, the Lalique Lady competition is over, the girl's been chosen, and I'm overdue for that vacation you promised me. I'm off tomorrow. So I'll be out of Sue's hair for a while. By the time I get back she'll have calmed down, and I'll keep well off her territory from now on, I promise."

The editor enjoyed his job, but not when he had to act as adjudicator in interoffice squabbles. "Fair enough. Leave a contact address. Going abroad?"

"No," Mel said sweetly. "Just planning a few days in Kent."

The editor cast a look of deep suspicion at her. "Kent? You haven't had a tip-off about anything to do with the Battling Brolly, have you?"

"Miss Seeton? Not a word. Now, I ask you, would I keep anything juicy to myself?"

"Damn right you would. Go away, Mel; you're making my indigestion flare up. And get in touch the moment she makes a move."

chapter
~4~

WENDY SMITH was in Bermuda, sitting at a poolside table with a really groovy man—the older type, graying at the temples—and sipping a daiquiri when the sound of a distant but approaching fire engine's bell unsportingly transformed itself into the shrilling of her alarm clock. She had bought it at the staff discount price at Woolworth's in Holloway Road eight or nine months earlier, and though of small intrinsic value it was one of her most important possessions. Wendy was nineteen, going on twenty, and she slept soundly. Too soundly, she soon discovered after she took the plunge, braved her dad's noisy bluster, her mum's tearful reproaches, and her younger brother Terry's hurt, uncomprehending silence, left the council flat near Shepherd's Bush for good, and moved in with her best mate, June.

June was a student nurse at the Royal Northern Hospital, but then she had always been brainy at school. Wendy admired her a lot, while preferring not to hear about the horrible yucky things she had to do in the line of her chosen profession. All the same she jumped at the chance of sharing the flat just off Seven Sisters Road, ten minutes' walk from the Northern, and a bit nearer than that to Woolie's. Since June had found the flat originally through the good offices of the lodgings lady at the hospital, she was really in honor bound to try to replace her departing flatmate with another nurse; but blow that, she had reasoned when offering the room to Wendy.

Wendy thought then that it was a terrific idea, and—apart from the row at home, of course, and the fact that she no longer had Mum to get her up in the mornings—she still did. She had been working at the Woolie's branch at Hammersmith since leaving school, and Mr. Turnbull had been really nice about arranging for her to transfer more or less straight away to the big one in Holloway Road. Their basement flat in the damp Victorian house wasn't exactly classy, but Wendy and June each had a bedroom, the kitchen was big enough to sit around in, they had their own titchy bathroom and toilet, their own front door!

Wendy's groping hand finally found the alarm clock and shut off the racket. Still half-asleep, she was briefly tempted to roll over and try another daiquiri in Bermuda. She had never been to Bermuda, never tasted a daiquiri, and actually didn't much fancy older men, but it had been an out-of-sight dream all the same. A few seconds later she came to full consciousness and the awareness that reality was currently much more fab than any stupid old dream; and she lay there for a minute or two wide awake and hugging herself in ecstasy. Could it be true? Was it really true? Yes, it really and truly was really and truly true! Good old Harry! Wow!

Having realized that she was positively looking forward to getting up, Wendy did so, and skipped into the kitchen in her baby-doll pajamas. There should have been some corn flakes left, but June must have noshed them before going to bed. Couldn't blame her really; must be the pits to be on nights. And there was still one Weetabix in the box, and half a tin of orange juice in the little fridge. These she dealt with on the wing, as it were, while moving her own and June's drying tights and knickers out of the way and running herself a deep bath with a fine disregard for the gas bill to come. Gas bills? Student nurses and girls who worked in Woolworth's might have to worry about gas bills, but Wendy didn't work at Woolworth's anymore, did she? Not since two weeks ago, two fantastic, unbelievable weeks ago!

Wendy lay back in the bath and happily reflected on her recent past. It had in fact been six months or so since she had met Harry Manning, early one evening soon after Christmas when she and June had been up the West End for the sales. They were in Regent Street, still giggling over some of the weird things they'd been looking at in Dickins and Jones, when this bloke in the hip leather gear and the fancy camera snapped their picture and then started chatting them up.

He claimed to be a freelance press, society, and fashion photographer, and this, Wendy remembered, had made them both fall about laughing. Harry was a good sport, though, and hadn't seemed to mind when June told him to pull the other one—it had bells on it. In fact, he took several more photos of them, together and separately, and the three of them ended up eating sweet and sour pork with rice and mixed Chinese vegetables in Gerrard Street. There Harry fished a tattered copy of *Nova* out of his capacious shoulder bag and showed them some pictures of glassy-eyed young people in evening dress. He said he'd taken them himself, at a ball at the Grosvenor House Hotel, and this time they believed him.

Harry insisted on paying for the meal, and before they parted he gave Wendy his card and asked for their phone number so he could let them know if—when, he said—

their picture was going to be in the paper. They hadn't got a phone, and Mr. Christodoulou in the ground-floor flat above them had made it very clear that he wasn't in the business of taking messages. June was a bit dubious about giving Harry their address, but Wendy told him anyway.

It was June who came into the flat shrieking with delight a few days later clutching a copy of the *Evening News* opened at the page from which two pretty, booted girls in Laura Ashley dresses under shaggy afghan coats smiled out across three columns above a caption that said NEW YEAR SPIRIT IN REGENT STREET. Wendy popped out to the phone booth at the end of the street and rang the number on Harry's card.

Harry was out on a job, she was told by the bloke who answered, and wouldn't be back till late. Any message? Oh, not really . . . well, perhaps just that Wendy rang to say we think the picture in the *Evening News* is really fab and thanks very much.

Needless to say it was all over both Woolworth's and the Royal Northern the next day, and the girls basked in the envious compliments showered on them. Then it all seemed to go a bit flat, until they got a note from Harry Manning on the following Tuesday saying he owed them a good dinner and what about some Italian nosh Friday, and to please give him a ring between six and seven Wednesday. Well, free dinners don't grow on trees, do they?

They both enjoyed the meal, and they both quite liked Harry, who seemed to know all the in crowd and had once been in the same room with Julie Christie *and* Terence Stamp. He smelled out of sight, too, and was wearing a different leather jacket, one that must have cost fifty quid at least. *And* he took them home in a taxi, sat in the middle but didn't try anything—well, you could hardly count a friendly arm round each of their shoulders and a good night peck.

All the same June was firmly against Harry's idea that they might make a useful bit of cash by doing part-time modeling work. Thanks, but no thanks. Harry Manning was quite old, must be going on thirty, and had been around—anybody could see that. Frocks and stuff for a mail-order catalog? Yeah, maybe, to start with. But then it would be bikinis, and then your boobs all over *Men Only* for the benefit of a load of dirty old men in raincoats, and then—no, thank you! But you do what you like, Wendy, no skin off my nose.

As she emerged rosily from the bath and reached for her towel—which could have done with a trip to the launderette round the corner—Wendy reflected that but for this fantastic, incredible stroke of luck June might have turned out to be right. Lying about in the cluttered little Camden Town studio Harry shared with his mate, Kevin, there certainly were plenty of, well, the sort of pictures that would give her mum a heart attack. You soon sort of got used to seeing them around, though, and began to wonder why teachers and clergymen and that Mrs. Whitehouse got their knickers in such a twist over a few tits and bums. Just like June'd said would happen.

June had not gone on to point out that the devil finds work for idle hands to do, but all the same it was true that after a few sessions in which Wendy had indeed modeled jumpers and skirts that might be all the rage in Macclesfield or Wolverhampton but which she personally would die rather than wear in public, other possibilities had suggested themselves to her.

To be strictly accurate, Lynn had suggested them. Wendy had met Lynn one day at the well-equipped commercial studio Harry rented for what he always called his "festive sprouts" fashion work, by which he meant cardigans, bed jackets, and the like for *Woman's Weekly*. It seemed that on one occasion a couple of his pictures had illustrated a feature "Adventurous Dressmaking" alongside one called "Party Food Need Not Cost a Lot." Included on the suggested menu was an item called "Festive Sprouts," and Harry enjoyed the thought.

Lynn was doing lingerie that day, and told Wendy how much she got paid: a good bit more than Wendy. Then, since something had gone wrong with the lighting and they were both kept hanging about with nothing to do but natter, it came out that Lynn also did glamor work and, you know, sexy stuff that paid even better. Wendy remembered how she had brooded about what Lynn had told her before broaching the subject with Harry, who looked at her with some surprise and hesitated before replying. Then he shrugged and said he reckoned she ought to stick to fashion, but there was no harm in banging off a few sample glamor pix if she liked.

Now, standing in her underwear in front of her dressing table mirror doing her makeup, Wendy remembered, too, the cringe-making embarrassment of that day in Harry's own little studio. It was bad enough in the bikini with her arms crossed to produce more cleavage, but when it came to the ones in the sexy gear she had herself bought at Weiss's in Shaftesbury Avenue, she nearly ran away. Yet Lynn had seemed such a nice, cheerful sort of person, somebody you'd enjoy going to the pictures with, and Wendy told herself that if Lynn could do it, then *she* could. So when Harry—coolly professional—told her to take off the wispy bra, she did, flaunted them, and even pouted her lips to order.

What a relief when, next time she went to Camden Town, Harry first gave her a set of prints that horrified her, then shook his head and told her to forget it. "You're a hell of a lot more curvy than Twiggy, love, and if you're hard up and willing to do anything for money, there're plenty of grotty types'll pay you for porn. But you've got the face to go upmarket. Fashion work, maybe really classy nudes one day, you know, David Bailey stuff, but not this sort of thing. You're learning fast. Be too good for 'festive sprouts' in a few months, but stick to it and wait for that lucky break. It'll come."

Come it did, thanks to good old Harry; Harry who heard on the grapevine long before it became common knowledge that Cedric Benbow had agreed to shoot a major glossy magazine feature and that the publicity types had dreamed up this notion of a nationwide competition to find "the possessor of The Face, the girl Cedric himself would select as his model and adorn with beautiful clothes and priceless jewels."

That was only the beginning. It had been Harry, and this pal of his, Mel, who had steered her through the preliminaries. Mel was pretty dishy herself but didn't exactly act like Harry's bird. Might have been, of course, but might not. Anyhow, she worked on the *Daily Negative* but said to keep quiet about that. Mel found out all about this Lalique geezer and located pictures of his stuff. Sort of weird, some of it, whopping great brooches looking like spiders or lizards and stuff, but some fab pendants, and bracelets, and things you'd hardly know how to describe. Really far out, anyway. Mel got hold of these photos of the sort of women who wore the jewelry, too. And picture postcards of paintings, like ads from fashion magazines, only real old. Lady This and the Princess de Wotsername. Actresses, too— Sarah Somebody and Lillie Langtry who used to have it off with the king, Harry said. And some bird lying on a heap of tiger skins in the nude except for about fifty bangles on her arms and legs and enough chains and necklaces to stock a shop. Dead kinky.

Wendy had a good giggle over the old-fashioned pinups and shook her head in disbelief, but Harry simply put a gentle hand under her chin, tilted her face upward, and looked at Mel, who nodded.

Transforming her hairdo at a classy Mayfair salon had cost a packet, but the makeup was just a matter of trial and error, until Mel was satisfied. Achieving the right facial expression was much harder. Wendy had already learned from Harry how to put on a toffee-nosed expression to order, but the women in the pictures Mel showed her looked kind of soppy, like they were trying to think up a poem about nightingales or something. June, who was absolutely super throughout the whole process and not a bit jealous, hooted with laughter whenever Wendy practiced her lovesick-cow look.

All the same, it worked. Harry must have taken hundreds of pictures, and from them he eventually put together a portfolio that took Wendy's breath away. Mel approved, too, and pointed out that she ought to have a name to match the new image. The one they all finally agreed on must have appealed to the judges in the two preliminary stages as well, because Wendy made first the long list, then the short list. So it wasn't as Wendy Smith the Woolworth's assistant that she was admitted, her legs feeling as though they had turned to jelly, to the presence of the great Cedric Benbow on that day of days. Nor was it as Wendy Smith that she later faced a battery of cameras, including that of good old Harry, who was grinning like a maniac, and saw herself later on in some of the papers and weekly women's magazines.

That, of course, was as the woman whose reflection now looked back at her from the cracked mirror of the dressing table in the grotty flat off Seven Sisters Road. The woman who would shortly be leaving that flat to go and stay at some unbelievably posh hotel for the next couple of weeks at *Mode*'s expense and who might very well, if things worked out the way Harry said they ought to, be returning only for as long as it took to find and move into a smart new flat of her own. In Mayfair, perhaps.

Yes, she was quite ready; the new dress suited her like a dream, and—a quick look out of the window told her—that must be the hired car just pulling up outside. Wow! Wendy Smith flung open the basement door, but it was the exquisite Marigold Naseby who floated up the steps to the street.

Just under half an hour later that morning, as Marigold Naseby palely and beautifully drifted through the doors of the Dorchester as if she had been accustomed to doing so since early childhood, Miss Emily Seeton reached the quiet lane and the tidily trimmed hawthorn hedge that bounded the northeastern part of the grounds of Rytham Hall. She was on her way to call on Lady Colveden. By appointment, of course, even though dear Lady Colveden had stressed that punctuality was of no consequence whatever.

"Oh, any time, any time. Elevenish or so? Whenever you're ready for a cup of coffee. I shall just be puttering about, you know. Deadheading, if it's another nice day. And George will be in Ashford dispensing justice, so he won't be underfoot and we'll be able to have a good chat. It's ages since I've been to one of these beanos at the palace myself, but they do tend to stick in the mind. I can still see old Tilly Trumpingham in that extraordinary frock going on at some bishop or other, positively *reeking* of mothballs. Tilly, I mean, not the bishop, but I don't suppose he noticed. Probably thought it was incense. I shouldn't think the drill's changed much in the past few years, so I expect I can give you a fair idea what to expect. Such fun the three of us are going . . ."

Well, elevenish or so is what Lady Colveden had said, and a quarter past eleven it would be. Rytham Hall was much less than a mile from Sweetbriars, not even a half

hour's walk on a lovely day like this, but Miss Seeton had
prudently allowed herself a good forty-five minutes so as to
be able to pause from time to time if anything in the way of
a bird or a flower needed to be appreciated. The thought of
actually going to the Buckingham Palace garden party was
still somewhat daunting, but the Kent countryside in July
was better than any tranquilizer.

The slowness of her progress gave Miss Nuttel and Mrs.
Blaine, who had of course seen Miss Seeton set out, plenty
of time to follow her and keep her in sight while they
themselves remained mostly concealed. They were still
deeply suspicious about the envelope with the royal coat of
arms on the back, and frequently discussed the matter,
agreeing that until it was satisfactorily explained, the only
thing that could be done was to keep a close eye on the
movements of "that woman."

It was after Miss Seeton had turned right into the lane
and rounded the next bend, with a hundred yards or so to
go to come to the Rytham Hall lodge gates, that she saw
the foot appear through the bottom of the hedge a few
yards ahead. Being tidy-minded, Miss Seeton at once corrected herself. To be strictly accurate, it was a shoe, but the
fact that an ankle was also visible made it a case of "foot is
understood," as her Latin teacher might well have put it
over half a century earlier.

Miss Seeton stood and watched a second shoe—also
complete with ankle—appear. They were good-quality
shoes, that much was clear at once, and quite suitable for
country wear, if hardly robust enough for hedge-crawling.
Soon most of their wearer's legs also came into view, and
these were clad in fawn cavalry twill trousers, which would
undoubtedly need to be sponged and pressed, if not dry-
cleaned, after their ordeal.

Miss Seeton could not imagine why a respectably
dressed gentleman should wish to emerge from the grounds

of Rytham Hall at that point and in such a complicated manner when there was a perfectly good driveway a little farther down; but having no wish to intrude, she prepared to move on. At this moment, however, the recumbent figure made a strange sound. It sounded like something between a muffled imprecation and a grunt of pain, and was accompanied by a thrashing of the legs and the appearance of an arm and hand, the latter scratched and bloody.

Filled with concern, Miss Seeton quickly approached the sufferer, tucked her umbrella under her left arm and stooped to render assistance. All she said was "Dear, dear, such a nasty scratch. Do let me help you," but the effects were dramatic. With a convulsive heave and a pitiful yelp the man shot backward out of the hedge and twisted his head round in such a violent way that he almost impaled his neck on the ferrule of the umbrella, which in fact became lodged between his collar and the knot of his necktie. Miss Seeton did her best to pull it free, but for several seconds succeeded only in creating a tourniquet effect and watched with alarm as the man flailed about wildly, his face becoming suffused with blood and his eyes bulging alarmingly. After what seemed a very long time he managed to grab the umbrella from her and wrench it free, after which he lay there for some time, shuddering.

From a safe distance the Nuts looked on in horror, Mrs Blaine clutching at Miss Nuttel's arm for security.

"Is he dead, do you think?" she quavered.

Miss Nuttel made no reply at first, but stared with narrowed eyes at the prone figure over whom Miss Seeton was stooping. "Not quite, it seems. I can see the poor fellow twitching," she said eventually.

"Oh, *Eric*! Death agonies?"

"Probably. I have never in my life seen such a vicious unprovoked assault, even on the television."

"Shouldn't we go and try to save him?"

"Out of the question, Bunny. In the first place he's almost certainly beyond medical help, and moreover it's sheer folly to approach an obvious homicidal maniac. Any policeman will tell you the same thing—oh. He's getting up."

"Oh." Mrs. Blaine sounded slightly regretful, too. "What shall we do?"

"Straight back to the village, of course. Find Constable Potter and report an attempted murder. He's a simpleton, but it should be possible to make even him grasp the seriousness of the situation."

chapter

~5~

"OH, POOR *chap*!" Lady Colveden said. "He must have been frightfully fed up about it."

"I'm afraid he was rather, yes."

"No wonder you seem a bit shaky. More coffee?"

"Perhaps in the circumstances, just *half* a cup, thank you so much."

"Um, Miss Seeton, I don't mean to be inquisitive, but why did you bring your umbrella with you anyway? There isn't a cloud in the sky." They were sitting in the conservatory, and Lady Colveden gazed thoughtfully out at the sun-drenched lawns.

"Do you know, that's almost exactly what the gentleman said. After he had recovered somewhat, that is. And wrapped a clean handkerchief round his hand. I explained that I never, couldn't possibly, go out without it. One never knows, and besides, it's the one Mr. Delphick gave me to replace . . . though of course I didn't mention that to the gentleman . . ." Miss Seeton's voice trailed away, and a touch of color appeared in her cheeks as she remembered

39

the circumstances in which the umbrella's predecessor had been wrecked beyond repair.

"Ah, well, bird-watchers are a law unto themselves, but strictly speaking he was trespassing anyway, so it served him right. A youngish man, you say?"

"Yes, and so beautifully turned out. At least, he must have been to begin with . . . after he was able to stand, and breathe normally again without making that awful whistling sound, he said it was all right, the tweed was thornproof. Very well-spoken, in spite of everything. But I'm afraid it wasn't, you know. Thornproof, I mean. One sleeve was ripped in two places, but invisible menders are awfully clever, aren't they? Perhaps he'll be able to get it repaired. His binoculars were undamaged, at least, and I expect that was more important to him than the state of his clothes. And naturally wavy hair."

Lady Colveden was inured to her visitor's afterthoughts and firmly steered the conversation back on course. "He calmed down eventually, then?"

Miss Seeton sighed. "Well, he *seemed* to. It must have been a great shock to his system, of course, so it's hardly surprising that he decided to go and look at birds somewhere else. I can't imagine where his car could have been parked without my seeing it, because he hurried off in the direction I had come from, and then in no time at all drove past me at what I must say struck me as excessive speed. I waved at him in the hope that there were no hard feelings, but he probably didn't notice. I hope that was the reason, anyway, because of course I had intended only to be helpful and only noticed the feet by chance in the first place. The shoes, that is. So I came to the conclusion that he must be hurrying off to find a chemist's shop. Quite unnecessary, because I had told him while he was recovering that Dr. Wright's clinic was quite close, and also that Mrs. Stillwell at the post office stocks iodine, lint, and sticking plaster."

"Never mind. All's well that ends well, as George would undoubtedly point out if he were here. I think Nigel's about the place somewhere, getting in the way of the people from the magazine. So *many* of them and for such ages, and all so that Cedric Benbow can mince about and take a few snaps. Nigel will be happy to run you home after we've sorted out the drill for Buck House on Thursday week. Unless I can persuade you to stay for lunch?"

"Too kind, but no, no, thank you. And I'm not sure I can take in what you tell me this morning, in view of—"

"Nonsense, nothing to it. George has already decided to have a hire car, so we'll all be going together, and once we're inside, all you have to do is enjoy yourself anyway. George and I certainly intend to: this place will be a madhouse for the whole of that week, I gather. Now, so far as a hat's concerned, the one you have on would be entirely suitable."

"Really? I'd thought perhaps a new one. But in the same style. It's rather interesting you know, he was called Clive when I knew him."

"Completely up to you. And white gloves, of course. Who was called Clive?"

"Cedric Bennett. Benbow, I mean. Cedric Benbow was called Clive Bennett. At art school."

"Why?"

Miss Seeton blinked. "I'm sorry, but I don't quite . . . ?"

"Why was he called Cyril Bennett?"

"He wasn't. He was called *Clive* Bennett. Because . . . well, that was his name, you see. He suffered from acne."

"What a funny chap. I could understand him trying Germolene or something, but I can't for the life of me see what good he thought changing his name would do. Anyway, we'd better get on. Buckingham Palace. As I remember it, there's always such a mob that they use two or three entrances to the grounds. We should get our admission tickets in a day or two, and they'll tell us which gate the driver should take us to. And then, inside, you just sort of mill about, look at the flowers, see if you can see anybody you know or spot somebody famous, listen to the band, make for the marquee, and try some of the delicious little petits fours they offer you."

"But . . . but, what about *Her*? Meeting, you know, Her Majesty?"

"Oh, good heavens, not a chance! Not unless you want to spend most of the afternoon trying to work your way through a rugger scrum, that is. Might *see* her with a bit of luck, in the far distance. Or one or two of the other royals doing the rounds. Oh dear, I do hope you aren't disappointed."

"No, no, indeed not. Quite the reverse. The thing that was making me most nervous is that, you see, I have no idea what one is supposed to say . . ."

"Well, mind you, I'm not saying it *couldn't* happen, but if by some remote chance it did, by the time you'd curtsied and said 'Yes, ma'am, delightful weather,' it would all be over."

"Really? That *is* a relief, I must say."

"Oh, look, here comes Nigel now. I do wish he didn't always look as if he's about to come in through the French windows and say 'Tennis, anybody?' Still, I should be thankful, really."

"Yes, I really think you should, Lady Colveden," Miss Seeton said firmly. "And proud, too, if I may say so. Nigel is a gallant, courteous, and considerate young man."

Lady Colveden smiled at her. "Thank you. That's a very nice thing to say." The smile became conspiratorial. "And a very susceptible young man, you might have added. Has he told you about Marigold?"

"Why, yes, he has. I understand she is very beautiful."

"Well, your friend Cedric Benbow or whatever he calls himself thinks she is. And so do a lot of other people, it seems. I haven't met her yet, but I've been shown some very clever photographs. I'm dying to see what she's like in person."

Chief Inspector Chris Brinton took off his glasses, rubbed his eyes, replaced the glasses, sat back in his chair, and laced his fingers together across his ample chest. "For lunch today I had a ham and tomato sandwich, well, two actually, and a pint of shandy because it's so hot. One pint, Foxon. Definitely just the one. So I'm sober. What on earth did *you* have?"

"Chicken, chips, and beans, sir. Bread and butter, strawberry milk shake, and a custard tart."

"Cripes, no wonder you've gone barmy."

"No, sir, got a touch of heartburn, but otherwise all my faculties, such as they are. Just reporting word for word what Potter said on the phone from Plummergen."

"Then it must be Potter who's blown a gasket."

"More likely that precious pair they call the Nuts, if you ask me. Mrs. Blaine and Miss Nuttel. They're the ones's reported the so-called incident. Potter got on his bike and went up there right away, but not a soul about in the lane, needless to say."

"Attempted *murder*? Miss *Seeton*?"

"That's what they alleged, sir. Vicious unprovoked attack with her umbrella on a defenseless man. Apparently she'd already felled him somehow before the Nuts were near enough to see. Man was lying there cringing from the blows. Then she throttled him, but didn't quite make a thorough enough job of it, because they said he seemed to be regaining consciousness when they ran off to tell Potter."

"Foxon. Listen to me. Miss Emily Seeton is what, in

her late sixties? She weighs about six or seven stone in her heavy walking shoes, I should reckon. And Scotland Yard pay her some piddling retainer as an occasional expert consultant. Now I'm consulting you, Detective Constable Foxon. Can you think of a single convincing reason why we should not charge those two silly cows Blaine and Nuttel, whom we know of old to be malicious gossips, with wasting police time? At the same time tipping Miss S. the wink on the quiet? To consider clobbering the old bags in the civil courts for slander, I mean?"

"Yessir."

"You *can*? A convincing reason?"

"Yessir. Umbrella, sir. I can see the headline: BATTLING BROLLY STRIKES AGAIN."

Brinton took off his glasses again, buried his face in his hands, and groaned. Then he looked up wanly. "I hate you, Foxon," he said, "but you could be right, blast your eyes. One way and another Miss S. has wrought more havoc in a few years with that confounded brolly than a man twice her size could with a stick of gelignite."

"Don't forget the Orac— er, Mr. Delphick gave it to her, sir. I think he sees it more as a modern version of Excalibur than a stick of gelignite."

"Nobody's perfect, Foxon, not even Chief Superintendent Delphick, and don't be such a bloody show-off. Excalibur my foot. You'd better get over to Plummergen and have a word with Miss Emily D. Seeton. God only knows why, but she seems to like you. Find out what, if anything, she used her umbrella for this morning, and ask her where she buried the body, if any. Oh, and drop in at Dr. Wright's place and see if Bob Ranger's turned up in the village yet, will you? The Oracle's organized a spot of leave for him so he can do some courting and keep a discreet eye on this fashion circus for us at the same time. Fill Ranger in if you see him. Just in case the Battling Brolly's latest victim tries to get his own back. I reserve the right to feel the collars of the Nuts at some later date."

Sir Sebastian Prothero winced as he did his best to achieve a reasonable effect with his black tie, but in spite of repeated efforts the end result was a sorry sort of butterfly compared with the perfection that normally set off his dinner jacket in the evenings. This was because he had not only ricked his neck in the course of the desperate struggle to free himself from Miss Seeton's umbrella, but had also strained his shoulder in extricating himself from the hawthorn hedge. Thank heavens his face was unmarked. The scratches on the back of his hand still looked red and angry, but could, he thought, be explained if necessary as the work of a temperamental cat. They smarted horribly, but nothing like as much as the outrage to his pride.

The thought of having been physically overwhelmed and so thoroughly demoralized by a dotty old woman who wasn't even trying was utterly mortifying and would, he knew, take him a long time to banish from his consciousness. The maddening thing was that until the mad old biddy had materialized from nowhere and startled him into that fatal movement, the trip to Plummergen that morning had promised so well.

So many and varied were his contacts that it had been simplicity itself to find out when the lighting people planned to go to Rytham Hall to join the features editor of the magazine and Cedric Benbow's factotum to examine the William Morris rooms in detail and work out what equipment would be needed and when. Prothero had intended to take advantage of the fact that a number of people more or less unknown to the Colvedens would be wandering freely about the place, and make his own leisurely reconnaissance. The cavalry twill trousers, hacking jacket, finely checked shirt, and quiet woolen tie would be sufficient in the way of camouflage: if they noticed him at all the fashion people would assume he was something to do with the family, and the family would think he was connected with the magazine.

If only he had stuck to that elegantly simple plan! Variants on it had served him so well in the past, when he had been planning break-ins at country houses whose owners he had known to be away. His expensive but well-worn casual clothes, his authentic upper-class accent with its echoes of Sandhurst, and his easy, charming but ever so slightly arrogant manner had taken in many a resident housekeeper, not to mention initially inquisitive gardeners and even the occasional passing policeman.

Curse it! After leaving the car in that perfect little concealed clearing on the other side of the lane so conveniently close to the Rytham Hall lodge gates he should have gone straight up to the house as large as life, not tried to be clever and spy out the land first with the aid of his binoculars. And it had been little short of madness to allow himself to be lulled by the total absence of other traffic in the lane and a fair-sized gap low in the hedge to have wriggled right into the confounded thing. The only thing he could be in the least proud of was that in his extremity he had kept his wits about him and thought of explaining away the binoculars with the tale about bird-watching.

The old woman was obviously gaga anyway, doddering about with an umbrella on a day like that, so she probably hadn't listened. Too busy babbling about iodine and clinics. In fact, within half an hour she'd probably imagined she'd dreamed the whole thing. Prothero breathed deeply and forced himself to think calmly. It had been a minor tactical setback, nothing more, which had done nothing to undermine his broad strategic plan. Even if his neck and shoulder did hurt like blazes.

With some difficulty he looked at his watch, started to

nod, and then thought better of it when it sent a wave of agony through his head. Reg Cobb had warned him over the phone that it was likely to be a busy evening at the club. There'd been a message to the effect that Omar Sharif might look in, and if word had reached the paparazzi, they were going to have their work cut out.

Prothero sighed. He honestly wouldn't have minded staying home and watching TV for a change. Still, it wasn't as if it were Peter O'Toole or Oliver Reed they were going to be coping with; and he'd probably be able to get away soon after midnight.

That would be a good time to start working on the girl.

chapter
~6~

EVEN AFTER their train arrived at Charing Cross and Nigel Colveden masterfully led the way to the taxi stand outside, Miss Seeton, though looking forward very much to seeing the Lalique jewelry, still felt something of an interloper. One had, she reminded herself, already suggested several times that, great treat though it was for her, it would surely have been much more pleasant for Nigel to have been accompanied by a friend of his own age, and one could hardly go on saying the same thing over and over again, could one . . . ?

"How lovely, he's taking us along the Mall, so we shall go through St. James's Palace, shan't we. And on such an agreeable morning, too. It is so very kind of you to invite me today, Nigel, though I can't help thinking—"

"Now, then, Miss Seeton, not another word. My mother's already explained that she's got to preside over some area-women's institute thing, and frankly, can you see my father in a Bond Street gallery with a lot of art critics and fashion writers?"

48

"Well, quite honestly, no, but since they passed on their invitations to you, surely one of your friends . . . ?"

"And *I've* explained that the only person in the world I'd ask before you would be Marigold Naseby, and she's going to be there anyway, surrounded by a lot of publicity staff. So you'll be able to explain about Lalique to me *and* I'll be able to introduce you to Marigold."

"That will be very nice. A Northamptonshire family, presumably. What a foolish man Charles the First was, but then weakness and obstinacy so often go together, don't they? Tell me, how did you come to meet Miss Naseby originally?"

"In the last round of the competition. Of course, *Mode's* business manager started negotiating with my father ages ago and it was all fixed for them to use the house and gardens as the background for the feature, but I don't think my parents quite grasped just what would be involved when the time came. Anyway, as soon as my college term ended last month and I arrived home, Father told me he couldn't cope with all the fiddle-faddle, as he called it, and that he was putting me in charge of the business arrangements. Personally, I've been finding it great fun. Well, I've already mentioned the last round of the Search for the Lalique Lady." Nigel somehow contrived to pronounce the capital letters. "Once they were down to the last six, the publicity people said they wanted them all photographed in the same room if possible, so I agreed on the terms and booked them for an extra day."

He smiled dreamily as the taxi left Berkeley Square and turned into Davies Street. "The models arrived together in a minibus and they were all smashers, needless to say. But after I'd met them one by one it was no contest as far as I was concerned. Marigold is so, well . . . *so* . . . anyway, Cedric Benbow chose her, didn't he? Gosh, I still can't get over your knowing him. I say, I've just realized that it's very likely he'll be there as well this morning."

When he first arrived in England shortly before the war, the teenager Ferencz Szabo had thought it only sensible to put thoughts of his native city of Debrecen behind him as far as possible. He was clearly going to have to live on his wits, and given that the English seemed to regard all Central Europeans with the same mixture of uneasy sympathy and suspicious distaste, it seemed probable that he would do better with an English name.

Ferencz Szabo translated very neatly into the no-nonsense, salt-of-the-earth Frank Taylor, so Frank Taylor he became, and so he remained for a very long time. During the first few months, while he was humping furniture about in the Harrods depository beside the Thames, he was called all sorts of other names and teased about his halting English and thick accent. However, Ferencz possessed a forgiving nature, an excellent ear, and a quick intelligence, and by the time he joined the army his speech was barely distinguishable from that of his workmates.

As a private and eventually a sergeant (acting) in the Royal Army Service Corps, Frank Taylor achieved no military glory. He did, however, vastly increase his vocabulary and master a useful range of new accents. He could soon do Brummie and Scouse to perfection, and in the sergeants' mess of an evening Frank was often plied with free beer in return for reproducing with uncanny accuracy the confident barking of career officers with permanent commissions and the contrasting, timidly fretful woodnotes of "temporary gentlemen." He was a godsend to the entertainment officer, who enrolled him in the company concert party, and his impressions often brought the house down in the Naafi on a Saturday night.

By the time Frank was released many months after the

war ended he knew himself to be fitted for better things than rearranging furniture in Harrods depository. For a start, he knew a thing or two about the disposal of army surplus stores. Within a year, successful and perfectly legitimate deals in boots, tools, office equipment, and vehicles had netted enough money for him to move into classier junk via an antiques shop in Chelsea.

There he based himself contentedly for a time, cultivating his eye for quality and assiduously studying auction catalogs. Over the next few years his flair, general savoir faire, and increasing experience propelled him steadily upmarket until he was able first to buy an interest in a Bond Street gallery and then to buy out its original owner.

That was a great day for him, except for one problem: what sort of a name was Frank Taylor for a dealer in rare and valuable objets d'art? Ideal for running a hardware or bicycle repair shop in East Acton, no doubt, but hardly Bond Street style. Ferencz Szabo, on the other hand, was absolutely right. Frank Taylor therefore quietly disappeared and the single word *Szabo*—gilded, and in slightly modified uppercase Perpetua lettering—appeared on the rich dark green paintwork of the fascia of the Bond Street premises, whose show window rarely displayed more than one item. The new proprietor's original Hungarian accent had long ago disappeared from his impressive repertoire, but he worked at perfecting a reasonable copy of it, never failed to kiss his female customers' hands, and prospered mightily.

Concluding the deal with *Mode* magazine over the Lalique jewelry show was the most deeply satisfying to date of his many and varied achievements, and it was with justifiable pride that Ferencz Szabo stood near the entrance of his gallery, side by side with the editor of *Mode*, to welcome invited guests to the special press show.

Press show it was, and publicity was its object. It therefore had to begin at what Ferencz personally considered to

be the uncivilized hour of eleven in the morning, so that
the people from television and the evening papers could
meet their deadlines; but media free-for-all he had no intention of allowing it to become. The young women
checking invitations just inside the doors—which invitees
had been warned would be closed at eleven-fifteen precisely—had been selected for their looks and style, but an
extremely large security guard in uniform lurked behind
them to discourage aspiring gate-crashers, and a number of
equally formidable colleagues of his were watching over
the exhibits. Their services were instantly available in case
of need.

Security was of course a crucial consideration, though
both the Szabo Gallery and the magazine had been required
by the owners of the pieces to arrange full insurance cover
at vast expense, quite apart from paying a fee Ferencz preferred not to think about for the loan. Publicity was, however, the name of this game, and it did Ferencz's heart
good to see the crowd of people who had gathered outside
to watch and to speculate about what was going on. One
TV crew had already filmed the scene in Bond Street, and
the thought that his gallery's discreetly elegant frontage
would in all probability be seen by millions of viewers
added to his pleasure.

The fashion writers, art critics, and a handful of experts
from museums like the Victoria and Albert and so on had
been warned that their invitations were strictly personal to
themselves, and Cedric Benbow had himself chosen the
very few photographers to be admitted. This almost guaranteed the stirring up of a fury of competitive envy on the
part of those excluded, which could only bring about
highly satisfactory results in terms of coverage.

It was a pity the *Mode* features editor had insisted that
an exception must be made in the case of Sir George and
Lady Colveden, who in accepting had nominated their son,

Nigel, and a Miss Emily D. Seeton as their representatives. Making the arrangements with Sir George for the use of Rytham Hall for a full week of shooting had, she reminded them, been a tortuous, even harrowing business, and it was simply not on to offend the Colvedens at this stage. In any case, she had added in a calmer voice, Nigel Colveden was all right, very helpful actually; and no doubt this Emily Seeton girl of his was an appropriately decorative popsy. . . .

Wendy Smith cringed miserably in her corner of the big limousine until it was nearly at Bond Street, and then with a supreme effort forced Marigold Naseby to take her place. For crying out loud, it was only for an hour or so, Liz had exploded at her earlier. "Course you've got to go, you daft cow, and watch that mascara! Don't feel well? Hoo, hark at her! Matter, got the curse or something? Well, that's what they call Sod's Law, innit? Think of it this way, you look like a dying duck in a thunderstorm already, exactly the way that old queen Benbow wants, so you won't even have to work at it this time. Just keep it that way and you'll have Hollywood on the phone by teatime."

Liz was a freelance makeup artist, engaged by the magazine to take care of Wendy's appearance for the duration of the project, and Wendy thought she was terrific. She knew all sorts of juicy scandal about famous people, for a start. She was full of beans that morning, excited about the do at the gallery and keeping up a steady flow of chatter while looking out of the window on her side of the car. But it was all right for her. It wasn't Liz who had answered the phone in the suite at the Dorchester well after midnight and heard that quiet, insistent voice.

It had taken a while for what the man was saying to begin to sink in. When it did, Wendy told herself to slam the receiver down, but by then she was feeling like one of

them rabbits caught in headlights and too scared to run
away. He wasn't a heavy breather, not like that creep they
finally caught at Shepherd's Bush—the one whose kitchen
window overlooked the Smith bathroom, and the coppers
worked it out that even with the curtain drawn like it
always was he could see shadows when the light was on.
No, he hadn't said anything crude. Nor was he what you
could exactly call smarmy, even when he was going on
about her face, a lot of fancy stuff about classic Fan De
Sickle looks or something. He sounded sort of cold and
snooty, like he could take it or leave it.

That was what had made it all the more horrible when
he'd started going on about these friends of his. Alfie,
Uncle George, and the Slicer. And how the Slicer's missus
had been having it away with some bloke and the Slicer
came home unexpected, and . . . and well, it was afterward
they'd started calling him that. But this scary man on the
phone said it needn't come to that, need it, because the
famous Marigold Naseby would be glad to do him a little
favor, and as long as she did he certainly wouldn't go in for
crude threats about telling the Slicer she was his girlfriend
and had been playing around.

What's more, if she was to do him this little favor he'd
give her a really nice present: the negatives of these photos
he had of her. You know, intimate photos. The photos and
the negatives, the lot. Otherwise . . . well, there were all
sorts of possibilities, weren't there, Miss Naseby. Apart
from the Slicer, of course, who had this thing about girls
who played around.

Certain newspapers would pay a lot for those photos,
and they'd print them like a shot, and Cedric Benbow
wouldn't like that one bit, would he? Probably call off the
whole project, indeed, and bang goes Marigold Naseby's
career as a top fashion model. Anyway, that was all hypo

. . . hypocritical or something. Meaning it need not happen, and once she'd had the nature of the little favor explained to her and seen how simple it was, she could set her mind at rest, couldn't she?

The limousine drew up outside the Szabo Gallery and somebody opened the door. In a trance of sick despair Marigold Naseby somehow managed to step out of the car, brave the cameras outside the gallery, and then go in. Liz followed her, a look of concern on her own cheerful, freckled face. The kid looked great, absolutely great, but there really was something wrong with her, Liz decided. Something worse than a bad case of stomach cramps.

Miss Seeton was obviously far from being the decorative popsy the features editor had envisaged. She was, however, by no means the only lady of mature years at the show, nor was she the least fashionably attired among them. She was outdone in the latter respect by a formidable expert from a museum in Austria who liked to be addressed as "Doctor Doctor," and by a remote, fey-looking woman in vaguely ethnic draperies smelling strongly of stale biscuits.

Moreover, Miss Seeton was in no sense a fish out of water in the Szabo Gallery. When in London for the day, she usually visited the Tate, the National Portrait Gallery, or one of the other collections, and knew very well how to comport herself. That day she was, as always, neatly and unobtrusively dressed. Nigel had been afraid that she might make a fuss when deprived of her umbrella on arrival, but Miss Seeton was quite used to surrendering it when visiting museums and art galleries and had handed it over at the improvised cloakroom quite meekly in return for a numbered ticket.

Now she was, there was no doubt about it, enjoying

herself very much. Especially after the glass of delicious champagne that the charming Hungarian gentleman had insisted on her taking. The only odd thing was that nobody except herself seemed to be showing the slightest interest in the Lalique jewelry. Even Nigel seemed to have drifted off somewhere while she was explaining why the William Morris rooms at the hall would be such an appropriate setting for the great man's work. Always supposing, of course, that the clothes Miss Naseby was to wear were sympathetic.

The dress she had on that day was perfectly splendid, but not perhaps *absolutely* right for Lalique. It must have taken two or three dozen yards of handprinted silk in a rich mélange of subtle forest colors to produce the great full sleeves and skirt. There was lace at the simple V neck, and on top of everything a little open jerkin in dusty pink and ivory, and by way of both hair decoration and garland a tangle of flowers, ribbons, and marabou feathers that made one think of Ophelia. The horizontally striped stockings that peeped out below the skirt suggested Tenniel's Alice, though.

Poor Nigel! It seemed most unlikely to Miss Seeton that he would have an opportunity to speak to Miss Naseby himself, much less be able to introduce them. She was in such demand. Never mind, she was in clear view most of the time and Miss Seeton always preferred if possible to form an impression of someone from a distance and in her own time. The child was indeed beautiful—or perhaps it would be more accurate to say that she had been made to look so. The features were good but not extraordinary, and it was the styling of the hair and the makeup that really gave her such a convincing Lalique look. That and the expression on her face. Whoever had coached her had done well, but someone should explain, or show her from paint-

ings, the difference between gentle pensiveness and with-
drawal into a private dream. Whatever sort of dream could
it be?

Miss Seeton edged a little closer to the group surrounding Marigold Naseby so as to get a clearer view of her
eyes, and what she saw in them troubled her. The poor girl
really did look quite faint, but then it was very hot and
noisy in the crowded gallery. That wasn't all, however. She
looked not so much distrait, which would be understandable for one not previously used to being so conspicuously
the object of attention, but *haunted*. Ought she to warn
Nigel? Suggest that Miss Naseby should withdraw to a
quiet room, an unoccupied office perhaps, to enable her to
compose herself?

She turned round to look for Nigel and inadvertently
bumped into a tall, aristocratic-looking man who was
standing just behind her, deep in conversation with Cedric
Benbow, who was wearing a panama hat and a cream-
colored raw silk suit with a pale blue ruffled shirt and a
darker blue cravat. Miss Seeton had earlier noticed Benbow at the far end of the room, and marveled even from a
distance at the transformation the years had wrought in
him. She had followed his glamorous career with interest
and had seen enough photographs of him to know what he
looked like as a celebrity. Suddenly finding herself at his
side quite disoriented her, though, and she clutched at his
sleeve in agitation.

"My dear Clive, I'm so sorry—I mean Cedric. That is,
Mr. Benbow. I do apologize for interrupting, but that poor
child is about to faint, I think. So very vulnerable . . . oh,
dear, of course you wouldn't remember me, would you?"

Benbow looked down with distaste at the little hand on
his sleeve and detached it fastidiously. Then he turned his
head and surveyed Miss Seeton. "You have the advantage

of me, madam," he said. "I'm afraid I don't recall the pleasure . . . nor do I have the slightest idea who you're talking about."

"She's right, you know," the other man cut in. "She means the Naseby girl. Very green about the gills. I'll go over."

"So kind." Miss Seeton smiled at him gratefully and watched him plow through the knot of people surrounding Marigold Naseby. Then she turned back to Cedric Benbow, who was surveying her, one hand to his chin. "How very good of your friend," she said. "I'm afraid I could never have made my way through all those people."

"Why did you call me Clive? Should I know you?" There was a touch of South London in the voice now, very different from the supercilious drawl he had used a moment earlier.

"I'm so sorry, but I was rather worried, you see, and of course when we were all students we always *used* to call you Clive, but I do realize that—"

"*Emmy*! Little Emmy Seeton! Well, I'll be blowed!" It was pure South London now, and to her delighted astonishment and the great surprise of those nearby, Cedric Benbow seized Miss Seeton and kissed her on both cheeks.

"It took me a minute to place you; then I remembered the way you always used to lose track of what you were saying. I told you to sign up for one of those postal courses in memory training like Pelmanism, remember the adverts, Let Me Be Your Father? You never did, that's obvious." The pimply, eager boy he had once been momentarily grinned out through the cynical eyes of the aging poseur, but then retreated as Cedric Benbow remembered where he was. He also noticed that Marigold Naseby had disappeared and that his friend was returning. The drawl was back in place by the time the other man joined them again.

"*What* a lovely surprise. Ah, there you are, dear boy. Emmy, allow me to introduce my old friend Sir Wormelow Tump. Wonky, this lady has known me even longer than you have. We were at art school together." A quick glance at her left hand, then "This is Miss Emily Seeton."

chapter

~7~

SIR SEBASTIAN Prothero strolled down Bond Street in a mood of pleasant expectation, planning to be among the first members of the general public to see the display of Lalique jewelry at the Szabo Gallery. He had toyed with the idea of wangling himself an invitation to the private view. That was the sort of thing Raffles or the Saint would do, but he had somewhat reluctantly decided that there was no sense in asking for trouble by mingling with people, some of whom would almost certainly be involved in the Rytham Hall photography project. Besides, it might be even more amusing to join the rubberneckers outside the gallery watching the invited guests leaving, then drop in at the Ritz five minutes' walk away for lunch. The exhibition was due to open officially at two in the afternoon. Not all the pieces on show were destined to come into his possession in due course, but it would be pleasing to see what was on offer, as it were.

He'd timed it beautifully. Quite a little crowd had gathered, wondering no doubt who was the VIP about to emerge and be driven away in the huge limousine drawn up outside, its smartly uniformed chauffeur waiting to open the passenger door. Prothero joined them, and after a very short time was delighted to see Marigold Naseby appear in the doorway in all the glamorous glory that provoked an audible intake of breath on the part of the two young women standing immediately in front of him. What pleased him especially was that she looked deathly pale, and that she was ushered to the car by several agitated-looking people who managed to get in one another's way. Eventually the girl was safely installed in the car, and it glided away. Great. His phone call had obviously done the trick. She was terrified.

Hang on, though. Who the hell was that old girl just coming out of the door? It *couldn't* be, but it was, by crikey! The frightful woman who'd nearly throttled him and then babbled about sticking plaster. That blasted umbrella and all. Gazing round as though butter wouldn't melt in her mouth. What was she doing here? Who *was* she, for heaven's sake?

Prothero hastily dodged backward and sideways, turned his back, and pretended to be engrossed in the display of high-class leatherware in the shop next door. Thank the Lord she hadn't spotted him. At least, he didn't think she had. Too busy gassing to the young chap with her. All the same, it'd be wise to check up on her. Good, they'd gone off in the opposite direction. No real need to worry, of course. The old trout was so vague and dotty that she'd probably forgotten all about that crazy business outside Rytham Hall in any case.

"Ar. By that gap down the bottom there. Er, I wouldn't try that, not if I was you, Sarge. If you don't mind me saying so," P. C. Potter added hastily. He had a lively sense of his station and its duties, and the idea of promotion hadn't for years entered his head, much less the slightest inclination to attempt the exams that towered Everest-like between him and three silver stripes. Mrs. Potter and Amelia Potter agreed that the head of their household was wise to leave well alone careerwise, while their cat, Tibs, offered no opinion.

Potter therefore invariably treated Ranger—who was a frequent visitor to Plummergen in his capacity as the fiancé of Dr. Wright's diminutive daughter, Anne—with the respect he considered due his exalted rank. This respect was enhanced by the fact that he, Potter, stood a fraction over five feet eight inches in his socks and the senior man six foot seven, with a frame he was wont to describe in conversation as being like a brick garage, Mrs. Potter having taken strong exception to the word her husband had originally used in place of garage.

Detective Constable Foxon made no comment. Being from Ashford, he was wordly-wise, and was not impressed by mere sergeants, as such. He had indeed every expectation of becoming one himself within a year or two, and did not for a moment imagine he would stick at that level. He had seen a good deal of Bob Ranger in the past couple of years, and they got along together perfectly well. Nevertheless, he would rather have enjoyed watching the gigantic Scotland Yard man trying to explore a gap whose dimensions would have made even an adventurous nine-year-old boy pause for thought. It was therefore with a passing twinge of regret that he saw Ranger pause, shake his head, and stand up again.

"Must have been a slender sort of chap to get in there, let alone out again," he suggested.

Ranger grinned. "Must have been a very *little* chap to be laid out by Miss S.," he said. "Why, she's even smaller than Anne."

"That's as may be, Sarge," Potter ventured, "but she's

pulled a few funnier stunts than that in her time."

Ranger was so tall that by raising himself up on his toes he alone among the three was able to look quite easily over the thick hawthorn hedge. This he did for perhaps twenty seconds before responding. Then he addressed himself to Foxon. "You've got to admit he's right," he said. "Damn funny place to pick for bird-watching, if you ask me. She was sure about the bird-watching, was she? When you spoke to her that same afternoon."

Foxon shrugged. "Well, yes, but you know what she's like. Goes all round the sun to find the moon. She only had his word for it, of course. That and the binoculars. Very well-spoken geezer, once he got his breath back, she said. Good clothes, the sort huntin', shootin' 'n' fishin' types turn up in at point-to-points. What was left of them, presumably, after she and this hedge were both finished with him."

Ranger looked down at the scuffed Hush Puppies on his own feet and his polyester slacks and short-sleeve shirt from Marks and Spencer. Anne had never breathed a word of criticism of his clothes, but Ranger had eyes in his head and had begun to scrutinize his future father-in-law's wardrobe and make mental notes.

"Did you speak to the Nuts, too?"

"Be more accurate to say they spoke to me. At me. According to them he was a poor old man, old age pensioner very like, harmlessly communing with nature when Miss S. creeps up behind him and launches this savage assault on him with her brolly. Tries to defend himself, which does not a bit of good according to our Bunny and Eric. Miss S. obviously thinks she's done for him, well satisfied, then she's taken aback when the presumed corpse shows signs of life. At this point our gallant Nuts belt off to get hold of the long arm of the law here and leave it up to him to referee the second round."

Potter nodded sagely. "This old bike o' mine might not do for the Toor dee France, Sarge, but I didn't waste much time getting here. Even so, no Miss Seeton, no bird-watcher. No blood, neither," he added thoughtfully.

"By then Miss Seeton was drinking coffee with Lady Colveden over there in the Hall. No doubt about that. And I can think of two good reasons why there was no sign of her alleged victim. One, because apart from being all shook up, he was perfectly all right and sensibly decided to put a good distance between himself and Miss Seeton's umbrella; and two, because he'd been up to no good. Right, Foxon?"

"Right on."

"Did the Nuts offer *any* sort of theory as to why a retired art teacher on her way to visit Lady Colveden should have wanted to set about this innocent, or why he himself hasn't seen fit to complain?"

"Not really. No, I tell a lie. Several. Those two have theories like some people have mice. Why did she attack him? Because she's a homicidal maniac, because she's a witch—"

"Oh, Lord, not that one again!"

"Hang on, I've hardly started yet. Because she's in league with the Freemasons and this chap had been giving away their secrets, because she has friends at Court who send her secret messages—"

"They're off their trolley."

Foxon sniffed in scorn. "You're telling me? Of course they are. Even if they weren't to start with, living with either of them'd be quite enough to drive the other one round the bend. Nuts by name, nuts by nature. I know that, you know that, Potter here knows that. But I haven't finished yet. Why didn't the victim report the attack? Because he did die in the end, she disposed of the corpse, and some picnickers will stumble on it one of these days. Or on the other hand, perhaps he survived but is so terrified of Miss S. that he's lying low and hoping to goodness she thinks her mission was accomplished and will therefore lay off him in future, or—need I go on?"

"No."

"Didn't think so."

"Still want to find out who he was, though. Imagine your guv'nor Mr. Brinton does, too."

P. C. Potter had been listening to this battle of wits between the Titans with some awe, but now timidly intervened. "We got a description, Sarge."

Foxon rounded on him. "Which do you favor, Potter, the old age pensioner the Nuts pitied while Miss S. was giving him a knuckle sandwich, or the bird-watcher with the hoity-toity voice and the high-class threads?"

His irony was wasted on the honest soul. "Well, I reckon we'd do better to go by Miss Seeton, meself. She took him for a bird-watcher 'cos that's what he told her, see. But like the sarge said, he could have been looking through them glasses to spy out the land, like. On account of these here jools."

"Good thinking, Potter," Foxon said keenly, and Ranger scowled at him.

"Put a sock in it, Foxon. We've put it about in Plummergen that I'm on leave, but we all know I'm really on duty, and I'm as keen as Mr. Brinton is—and you should be—to find out as much as I can about any suspicious characters seen nosing about Rytham Hall. The magazine circus will be here in a couple of days and the sparklers soon after. Go on, Potter. I agree with you, but it's not much of a description, is it? Miss Seeton's, I mean. Upper-class voice, well dressed, probably getting on for forty and with wavy hair." Ranger turned briefly to Foxon. "She told Lady Colveden that as well as you." Then back to Potter. "Heck of a lot of people fit that description."

"Ar, very like, but Martha Bloomer told me this morning as how Miss Seeton's been at her sketching pad. Must have been after she got back from London yesterday evening. Young Nigel Colveden took her to see some exhibition. Seems to me as how she might have done one of them pictures of hers, what she does without thinking. Of this here chap in this here hedge."

Ranger smote himself on the forehead. "Good grief, it never even entered my head to ask her to draw—"

"An' what I reckon is," Potter continued remorselessly, for if it took him a while to get warmed up, it took him just as long to simmer down again, "that if we was to proceed to Sweetbriars now in a horderly fashion and ask the good lady to be good enough to let us have a look at them sketches, we might find what they call a speakin' likeness of this here chap." His two colleagues looked at him with unwonted respect.

"An' what's more," Potter added to clinch matters before finally subsiding, "I reckon we'll get a cup of tea and a bit of Martha's fruitcake."

Recognizing that the village constable had surpassed himself, Ranger nodded, Foxon nodded, and the three of them set off.

"Yes, I've got the photocopies in front of me now," Delphick said. "I'm more than grateful to you for sending them up by car, Chris. Extraordinary, aren't they? But then, her sketches always are. I wonder why she represented the fellow as a bird." The line from Ashford wasn't very good, and he strained to hear Brinton's reply.

"Because he said he was a bird-watcher? Yes, I follow your reasoning, but in my experience the lady's subconscious mind works in subtler and more mysterious ways than that. What we've got here isn't the kind of bird that frequents the hedgerows of Kent. It's more like the sort

that hovers over exhausted explorers in the middle of nowhere. What? No, the face doesn't immediately ring a bell
with our Rogues Gallery chaps, but they're working on it.
Look, Chris, this is a bad line, and I've got a queue of
people banging on my door. I'll get back to you. Thanks
again."

It wasn't strictly true that anyone was waiting to see
him. In fact, it wasn't true at all. Delphick simply wanted
to brood in peace over the photocopies of the sketches Miss
Seeton had handed over to Messrs. Ranger, Foxon, and
Potter. No doubt with the usual embarrassed protestations
that they were just ridiculous doodles, of no conceivable
interest to anyone.

Delphick smiled at the thought. There would of course
have been no question of her refusing: Miss Seeton had—
or gave the impression of having—only a very imperfect
understanding of the nature of the services she rendered to
Scotland Yard, but was clearly honored to be in their em-
ploy even if the computer did insist on addressing her
payslips to 'Miss Ess.' Not in Delphick's view that she was
paid anything like enough: just a small monthly retainer
and expenses when appropriate.

On the face of it, Miss Seeton's modesty about her
technical skills was quite justified. She knew her history of
art inside out, could draw and paint competently, and had,
Delphick knew, been a successful, even inspiring teacher
for many years. He had, however, seen a good many of her
own informal sketches and more carefully executed paintings and found them generally pleasing, but hardly ever
more than that. It was only when she was on automatic
pilot, as it were, that she produced the weird works of
genius she referred to dismissively as doodles or carica-
tures, the sketches that made Delphick stand in awe of the
depth and power of her imagination, and sometimes argue
to Sir Hubert Everleigh that she must be a true clairvoyant.

He wished he had the originals of the three now in front of him rather than photocopies. Fortunately, however, Miss Seeton had on this occasion used the clean, bold lines of the cartoonist rather than going in for any subtlety of shading, and the copies were entirely satisfactory for his immediate purpose. Delphick looked for a few seconds at each in turn, then began again, taking much longer the second time.

The first sheet had three drawings on it, all involving the mysterious bird-watcher. At the top of the sheet he was flying over a recognizable Rytham Hall, beside which stood a tiny but vividly convincing Sir George Colveden aiming a shotgun at him. The bottom left-hand corner showed the birdman at rest, perched brooding on top of a hedge from the bottom of which two human legs protruded. The biggest drawing occupied the center of the page, and was the most disturbing, for it vividly suggested that the creature was attacking the artist. It was a vulture-like bird; it was also a man, and a credible man at that, even with the nose grotesquely elongated into a beak and the fingers transfigured into talons.

The second sheet bore a single drawing only: of two elderly men in conversation, in the middle of a crowd suggested with uncanny effect by no more than a couple of scribbles with the charcoal. This sketch was in the manner of a *Spy* cartoon, the proportions distorted but otherwise conventional enough: the heads greatly enlarged and the bodies dwindling almost to nothing.

Delphick thought he recognized one of the faces as belonging to somebody famous. Who the devil could it be? Noel Coward? Somerset Maugham? Trevor Howard? No, not Trevor Howard. Howard's face was battered and cratered like the surface of the moon, certainly, but this chap —for some reason depicted in schoolboy shorts and holding a catapult—was more . . . got it! Benbow! Disfigured, and a far cry from the old smoothie whom he had often seen waffling away on television chat shows, but Cedric Benbow without a doubt.

Delphick hadn't a clue who the other one might be. Elegant, aloof, typical establishment figure. Clubman, but Carlton or Athenaeum rather than Garrick or Reform. Delphick peered more closely at the picture. Were this top person's fingers crossed behind his back? Yes. Now, why on earth should Miss Seeton have dreamed up a gesture like that?

Delphick turned to the third sheet, which again was given up to a single drawing, to him the most mysterious of the lot. Benbow and his companion again appeared— just their faces this time—among those of a number of other men evidently getting on in years, spectators apparently, or more probably voyeurs. For the picture was dominated by the figure of a nude girl. Head bowed, sorrowful but seemingly resigned, she was turned half away from the onlookers. She held a filmy drapery up to her right shoulder in such a way that it partially concealed her right breast and thighs, and appeared to be oblivious to the presence in the background of the birdman, now further transformed into something more like a lizard, or dragon perhaps, with a huge tail.

The picture made him feel depressed, and after pondering over it for some time Delphick turned back to the first sheet. The little caricature of Sir George in his riding breeches cheered him up no end. Miss Seeton had him down to a tee. It would be just like the old boy to take a pot at any nightmarish creature out of Hieronymus Bosch that presumed to invade his domain.

chapter

~8~

"FOR PETE'S sake stop saying over and over again 'How *could* you, Harry?' I've already told you I didn't, and if you don't believe me, I'm going to put this phone down right now. Okay? Now stop grizzling and listen. It's possible Kevin might have done the dirty. I don't like saying it, but he's not above helping himself to loose change out of my coat pocket, and he's got a few friends I wouldn't trust further than I could throw 'em. If Kevin came across those negs in the filing cabinet, and you suddenly in the big time, well . . . I've had it out with him, anyway. He denies it, of course, says all sorts of people are in and out, and often on their own long enough to have a good rummage round. And I can't deny that's true. Anyway, whether he nicked those pics or didn't, we've busted up. I'm moving out and getting my own place."

"That's all very well for you, but what am I going to *do*?"

"Do? Tell this mystery man to piss off, that's what. Call his bluff. Listen, Wendy, I'm the guy who took those photos, remember? They're *nothing*. You can get mags full of pics like that and a hell of a lot stronger at any station bookstall."

"Not of Jean Shrimpton or Twiggy you can't."

Not for the first time, Harry Manning reminded himself that during the past few weeks a certain amount of Wendy Smith's naïveté had worn off. *Was* it so ridiculous now for her to see herself up there with models whose names were household words? Especially in view of this fantastic possibility that looked like it was coming her way? He ought to try to look at it from the kid's point of view.

"Yes, well, I can see how you'd be upset. You're right, some of the papers might pay a bundle for them. And that could muck up your career. Mind you, the *Mode* people have put so much into this project already that I can't see them dropping you at this stage whatever happens. But look, Wendy, if you won't tell me what this man's after, how should I know how you ought to handle it? What's he want? Lolly? Everybody says you should go straight to the fuzz if you're being blackmailed. Listen, I've just thought, Mel knows a pretty big cheese at Scotland Yard. I bet if you tell her about it she could—" He held the receiver away from his ear as a heartrending wail interrupted him.

"I *can't* tell Mel. And I can't tell you! I wish I could, but I *daren't*. Not till after, anyway, because of, well, just because, that's why. . . . "

Long after she had put the telephone down Wendy remained in the corner of the sumptuous sofa in her room at the Dorchester, curled up with a thumb in her mouth and wondering if it was all really worth the hassle. She would have given a lot to be back in their grotty flat, sitting in the kitchen with June and tucking into a biriani from the Moti Mahal takeaway near the tube station. S'pose she did tell the phone man to piss off like Harry said, and the photos got into *Men Only*? What was so great about *Harper's*,

Vogue, and the other posh glossies anyway? She bet *Playboy* paid just as much or even more, and some of those centerfold girls got offered jobs in pictures.

For a little while life seemed possible again, but then the all-too-familiar lurching sensation in her stomach returned as the vision of Alfie, Uncle George, and the Slicer swam back into her consciousness. Especially the Slicer. She hadn't met any of these friends of the phone man yet and devoutly hoped she never would, but they were with her every waking hour. She just somehow knew that Alfie was thin, scruffy, and furtive, a bit like that big brother of Wayne at school. The one who used to hang around when the girls were playing netball and stare at their navy blue knickers.

Uncle George was more like the fruit-and-veg man in the street market, fat and jolly, you'd think at first until you saw his little piggy eyes and his slobbery mouth when he took a nip out of the half bottle of whisky he kept in his pocket. Then there was the creepy way he always tickled your palm when he gave you your change. Yuck.

As for the Slicer, well, he was straight out of a horror movie. His features weren't clear in her mind because he wore one of those scary stocking masks that made his nose and lips go all squashy, but he was big and strong, and the open razor he carried glittered blue when the light caught it.

And oh, *Gawd*, never mind the papers, if she didn't do what he said, the phone man would put the Slicer on to her, and he'd get his jollies cutting her up, and if that happened, they wouldn't even have her back at Woolworth's, let alone the Playboy Club down Park Lane there. And the phone man would: you could bet your boots on that. He sounded so icy cold, ruthless, and confident. . . .

• • •

Sir Sebastian Prothero had recovered from the jolt he had experienced on seeing that mad old biddy coming out of the Szabo Gallery and now felt cool, laid-back, and confident. The first reconnaissance visit to Rytham Hall might have been a pretty fair disaster, but the second had more than made up for it. Before setting out he'd thought about ways and means of getting hold of a post office telephone van for an hour or two but then reminded himself that simplicity had always been the hallmark of his modus operandi. That, presence of mind, and a certain amount of cheek.

So, no nonsense, straight round to the back door this time, in the white overalls with a couple of screwdrivers in the top pocket and the old telephone handset from the electrical junk shop in Tottenham Court Road tucked under his arm. Pair of headphones sticking out of another pocket. A workaday voice for the benefit of the housekeeper: skilled man, but no toff.

"Morning! Colveden, Rytham Hall, right? Family all out? Never mind, no need to bother them. Several callers recently been having difficulty getting through, had to get the operator to help them. Quick check of the main phone and, let's see, two Plan Seven extensions, isn't it?

"Three? There they go again, those boneheads in records probably forget their own addresses half the time. Trouble you to show me all four? Thanks, but better if you don't mind being there, keep an eye on me, you know? Covers me, too, you see, anybody misses something and decides the phone man must have had sticky fingers. Shouldn't take more than ten or fifteen minutes all told."

In fact, just over eight minutes in all had sufficed for him to fiddle in turn with all four of the handsets in the house, nod wisely over them, and cause the master instrument in the hall to ring insistently. Another four minutes to memorize the layout, and then casually, "Right, seems okay now; give us a ring if you have any more trouble. I'll let you get on with your work now. Just have a glance at the outside wiring, then be on my way. . . . What? Nice of you; thanks all the same, but I had a cup out of my thermos just before I disturbed you. Ta-ra then."

All most satisfactory. Might have been tricky if it had been a case of going in there and lifting the jewelry. Impossible, really, for one man who worked alone because he believed if you wanted a job well done you should do it yourself. All right, this time he wasn't *strictly* working alone. Because that empty-headed little dollybird was going to drop tens of thousands of pounds worth of goodies out of the bathroom window, wasn't she? Because she knew what was good for her. Because she believed in bogeymen like Uncle George, Alfie, and the Slicer. Prothero thought the Slicer was definitely one of his better inventions, made up on the spur of the moment on his way back to his flat after acquiring those boring cheesecake photos.

Still, commonplace little tart though she might be, this girl who called herself Marigold Naseby was the best accomplice he was ever likely to have, and within a few days several priceless Lalique masterpieces would be in his possession. Then Phase Two would begin.

The chain-smoking Amsterdam jeweler who was his regular fence and knew him only as Henry had taught Prothero a lot. He knew quite well that museum pieces like the ones he was about to acquire were for all intents and purposes unsalable. They were nevertheless definitely negotiable, and Prothero looked forward very much to his forthcoming anonymous battle of wits with the insurance people. He could take his time; he didn't need the money particularly—he was just enjoying the awareness that he was smarter than the police. He'd made monkeys of several provincial forces already since deciding to become a gentleman burglar, and was in no doubt that he could do the same with the flatfoots of Kent.

"Chummy's getting too big for his boots," Chief Inspector Brinton said with grim satisfaction to Bob Ranger after the housekeeper at Rytham Hall had left the room, beetroot red with embarrassment. "That was a very bright idea of Potter's, to show her Miss Seeton's birdman. Saucy sod! Checking the phones, was he? I'll show him personally where he can put his screwdriver when I catch him."

"It's funny in a way, sir. Miss Seeton always refers to the work she does for us as 'drawing Identikit pictures,' whereas we've hardly ever actually asked her to. She has for all intents and purposes produced them from time to time, but we've never used them in the conventional way. And we certainly couldn't do it with this." Ranger pulled a face at the single sketch they had shown the housekeeper, to the poor woman's great consternation. It was the one depicting the grotesque bird perched on the hedge.

"Show it on the TV, you mean, print it in the papers, put up posters—HAVE YOU SEEN THIS MAN? No, you're right. The media'd fall about laughing, even though the housekeeper recognized his ugly mug right off. I can hear them telling us to try the zoo." He scowled, then brightened. "Get one of your regular police artists to adapt it, perhaps? You know, turn it into a normal sort of human phiz but keep the likeness?"

"Might be worth trying, I suppose, sir. But then on the other hand it could be both premature and counterproductive to go in for mass publicity. Chap hasn't committed any crime so far as we know—not yet, at least. He was seen looking through a hedge by the side of the public highway: tens of thousands of people do that every day. And it wasn't as if he broke in here. The housekeeper let him in and showed him round. And she stressed that he'd wanted her as a witness to make sure he didn't nick anything. Put his likeness in the paper, identify him by name, and he could have us in a very awkward spot, wrongful arrest, police harassment, defamation of character, you name it."

"All right, all *right*, Ranger, don't rub it in, man. Of course, the Yard can't say for sure that he hasn't got any form, but they've had a good look through a hell of a lot of mug shots and haven't come up with any known villain who looks remotely like this beauty. So what about you coming up with something we can do instead of pointing out all the things we can't?"

"It's Tump all right," Deputy Assistant Commissioner Fenn said. "With Cedric Benbow. Well, I'll be . . . needn't have gone to all that trouble to get her invited to Buckingham Palace, need I?"

Sir Hubert Everleigh regarded him blandly over the top of his glasses. "I must say you're easily pleased, old boy. Got all you want, have you? Trot over to Curzon Street— 'Here you are, my dear old MI5 chaps—open-and-shut case. Feller's obviously got a guilty secret: look at the way he keeps his fingers crossed.' I'd rather you than me."

"Ah. Yes, see what you mean. Rather convenient that she's going to get a second look at him next week. Better wait and see if she comes up with anything else, perhaps. Extraordinary, though, that she should have bumped into him like that."

"Not really. That picture's one of three. More than three, actually; three sheets, I mean. Produced by Miss Seeton when she got home from the Szabo Gallery in Bond Street. According to the Oracle she'd been to a private view there. I fancy I saw something about it in the *Evening Standard* myself."

"I wonder how Cedric Benbow and Wormelow Tump came to be there?"

"That's easily explained. Delphick told me all about it. It was one of those, what d'you call 'ems, media events. Apparently old Benbow's been hired by one of those glossy magazines women read under the hair dryer. You know, horoscopes, articles about Tuscany, adverts for fur coats and corsets—only my wife says they don't call them corsets nowadays. Benbow's going to take pictures of a lot of damn ridiculous clothes, fin de siècle look or something, and they're making a big thing of it. Borrowed a collection of priceless period jewelry from the Continent to go with 'em—the frocks, I mean. And the magazine got together with the Szabo Gallery people; share the expenses no doubt. Joint sponsors, special exhibition of the jewelry, very rarely on display, I gather. Couple of pounds to get in. Stuff like that's very much in Wormelow Tump's line, of course; hence they have him along there. Seal of approval, you see."

"Yes. Hardly Miss Seeton's style, though, I should have thought."

"Not ordinarily, no. But Benbow's going to take his pictures next week in Plummergen of all places, where Miss Seeton lives. Old George Colveden's giving the magazine the run of Rytham Hall. Cut a long story short, Colveden's a Justice of the Peace, golfing crony of the chief constable down there—what's his name?—Rupert something. Bit twitchy about having all this fancy jewelry on his premises, so Rupert—Rupert? No, Robin, perhaps—anyway, the Chief Constable passed the word down the line for an eye to be kept on the place."

"Yes?"

"What do you mean, yes? Haven't I made myself clear?"

"Not entirely, Sir Hubert." Following the ticking off to which he had been subjected when last in the assistant commissioner's office, the Special Branch man was treading delicately. "I mean, I don't quite see why the Oracle and Miss Seeton are involved."

"Delphick's involved because the fellow in charge at Ashford rang to ask his advice. Delphick's sergeant's engaged to the doctor's daughter in Plummergen, so he's well-known about the place, and the Oracle agreed to shunt him down there while the photography's going on. And Miss Seeton went to this private view because Colveden's son took her. Wait a minute: I've just realized your man Tump's in another one of her pictures."

Sir Hubert rooted through the papers on his desk, found Miss Seeton's drawing of the nude girl and the elderly voyeurs, and handed it over. Fenn contemplated it for a while in silence and then emitted a low whistle. "I say, bit near the knuckle for a retired spinster, isn't it?"

"Don't be an ass, she's the most matter-of-fact person in the world about nudity. She was attending life classes at art college long before you even started swapping dirty jokes at prep school. Doesn't stop her being a perfect lady. What do you make of it?"

"Well, it's an extraordinary picture by any reckoning. But it doesn't throw any more light on Tump, I'm sure you'd agree. Just his face; same sort of expression as the others gawking at her. Have we any idea who the girl is?"

"Yes, she's Cedric Benbow's model. Chose her himself it seems. Some sort of competition; thousands of girls applied. She was at the Szabo Gallery do as well. Not starkers, though, I need hardly add. That was just the way Miss Seeton saw her."

"Good likeness, though?"

"I think we can take that for granted. Pretty child, don't you think? Can't help feeling sorry for her somehow, can you?"

chapter
~9~

"OH, DO stop fussing, George," Meg Colveden said at last, with what was for her a rare show of exasperation. Her husband was sufficiently taken aback to lower his newspaper and look at her with raised eyebrows. "Nigel has everything under control, and after all, it was you who agreed to all this in the first place."

While inwardly recognizing the justice of her remarks, Sir George was enjoying his grumble too much to abandon it right away.

"Didn't bargain on a lot of poofters poncing about the place."

"Now, George, language! And in any case, you have no reason whatever to imply any such thing. I've found the people from the magazine quite delightful, and I'm very much looking forward to having Cedric Benbow as a houseguest. It's only for a few days anyway."

"Few days! To take half a dozen snaps! Good God, I could do it in ten minutes with my old box Brownie."

"Dad, your old box Brownie sat on the white elephant

stall at about six successive village summer fetes until some fathead eventually gave a couple of bob for it," Nigel pointed out. "I remember Ma warned me not to buy it back for sixpence the first year and I was about eight then. Couldn't get the film anymore."

Far from crushing his father, Nigel's intervention fanned the embers of his sense of grievance. "Couple of bob indeed! Feller got a bargain, I'll have you know. Saw one just like it in an antiques shop window in Canterbury last time I was there. They wanted a tenner for it."

"Oh. Yes, well, people do seem to be into nostalgia these days, I must admit. Anyway, that's not really the point, Dad. To get a dozen or so absolutely terrific pictures, Cedric Benbow will probably take several hundred." He paused, blushing becomingly. "And it'll take a lot of time for Marigold to change dresses and have her makeup and hair redone for each one."

Sir George reached for another piece of toast and looked at it in disgust. "Stone cold as usual. What sort of an idiot invented toast racks? They give it to you wrapped up in a cloth in decent hotels. Yes, but what's he want to *stay* here for? That's what I want to know."

"It's because of the outside pictures, dear. That very pleasant young man with the beard explained it all to me. Natural lighting, you see. We're enjoying a very nice settled spell of good weather, it's true, but of course we can't count on that for next week. It could easily turn out to be a case of seizing any opportunity that arises."

"And even if we do have a lot more sunshine, I imagine Benbow will want to try some early morning and some evening shots, Dad. You know, pearly dawn, romantic sunsets . . ." Nigel grinned and pretended to duck to avoid a parental assault. "So it makes sense for him to be on the premises, with Marigold and a few other key people nearby."

"Poppycock. Perfectly good pub in the village."

"Oh, really, George! Mr. Benbow is a very distinguished man. The George and Dragon wouldn't be at all suitable for him. Besides, it's fully booked. They've given Miss Naseby their best room, and Mr. Benbow's assistants and people from the magazine have the rest."

An old campaigner, Sir George knew when defeat stared him in the eye. "Good mind to give old Freddie a ring down there in Ross-on-Wye. Few days fishing might be the thing."

"I'd say that would be an excellent idea, except that you're forgetting the garden party at Buck House, dear."

Nigel waited politely to speak, until his father had finished groaning theatrically. "Why not go down there the following week, Dad? Recuperate after it's all over. Besides, you'll enjoy it while it's happening, you know you will. And you can lend a hand keeping an eye on the Lalique jewelry."

"So, very good," Ferencz Szabo said. "I shall close the gallery at eight o'clock. The representatives of the owners and the insurance company must be here well before then, of course. Then we shall together supervise the placing of each piece in its case, and the cases in the strongbox by the Securicor manager."

"Right," the *Mode* business manager agreed. "The same procedure as when the jewelry was delivered to you, only in reverse."

"Precisely, except, my friend, that I shall feel more joyful when I see you and the Securicor representative sign the documents than I did when it was my responsibility to do so."

"Don't regret it all, do you, Ferencz?"

"But no, not for a second! It has been a triumph! My little shop has always been on the map, of course, but from now on its name will be mentioned everywhere the critics meet, at every vernissage, every—"

"Right on. We're pretty pleased, too. My circulation manager's delighted. Pity young Marigold flaked out like that at the press show, but—"

"No no *no*! She did it so beautifully! And the *Guardian* critic mentioned that it was on the shoulder of no less a personage than the Queen's Custodian of Objets de Vertu that the sweet child swooned. Dear friend, you must cherish her; she will be worth her weight in gold to you from now on." Ferencz took an amber cigarette holder from his waistcoat pocket, inserted a dusty pink Sobranie cigarette into it, and admired the effect. "My security here is always very good, *bien entendu*. But you must have some anxiety about this country house, no?"

"No, not really. They'll only need a few pieces at a time, you see. Securicor will deliver the strongbox and take it away again in an armored van each day, and have a guard over it. Each piece Benbow wants to use will be signed for and then checked in again, needless to say. Big firm like that, I expect they've worked out very elaborate safeguards. Anyway, it'll be their worry, not ours."

"And most assuredly not mine." Ferencz beamed with satisfaction and finally lit his cigarette as the *Mode* man prepared to leave, then paused.

"Oh, I nearly forgot. Albertine said to mention that you'd be quite welcome if you felt like dropping in one day during the shooting. Long way to go, of course, but she thought it might amuse you to see the Lalique pieces actually being worn for once, and with the right sort of clothes in the right sort of context."

Miss Seeton had not really enjoyed the chicken salad Martha had prepared for her lunch before going back to her own cottage nearby. She suspected, quite rightly, that until very recently the poor chicken, like the lettuce, cucumber, and radishes, had flourished in her own rather large garden. In return for keeping the remainder tidy and for supplying her with eggs and with soft fruit and vegetables in season, Stan Bloomer had her full permission to keep hens in and cultivate well over a third of it. It was understood that he would sell whatever produce was left over after the Bloomers' own table had been supplied, pocketing the proceeds. The arrangement suited both parties admirably, and so far as eggs, fruit, and vegetables were concerned Miss Seeton had no scruples about enjoying her share to the full. Although she was not a vegetarian, however, the thought of the ultimate fate of the hens troubled her.

At least Mr. Bloomer was always scrupulous to deal with the more distressing aspects of the process when she was out, she thought, wobbling alarmingly but just succeeding in maintaining her balance. For in the privacy of her bedroom Miss Seeton was standing on her head, something she made a habit of doing, for a short time at least, every afternoon she was at home, after running through some of the less exacting postures described in *Yoga and Younger Every Day.*

All the same, the frequent appearance of chicken on her table did constitute a recurring moral problem. Perhaps without giving offense to either of the Bloomers she could explain that she had decided to go on a special diet that excluded chicken. She would, of course, have to honor her word—not that there could be any question of her *not* doing so—and do without chicken altogether from now on, even in restaurants and other peoples' houses, not that she dined out very often anyway. It would be a small enough deprivation, to be sure.

Miss Seeton continued to muse about diets after she finished standing on her head and managed to assume the lotus posture. The pain was undoubtedly diminishing with practice, yes, but it would be very nice to be able to walk normally again in less than half an hour after doing that particular exercise. Perhaps a diet might even help. People were advocating some really quite unusual diets these days, avocado, grapefruit and so on, though hardly yet the Diet of Worms! Birds were widely supposed to live on worms. Even hens might eat the occasional worm, perhaps, given the opportunity, and they were undoubtedly early birds of the kind said to catch them.

Now, why should she suddenly think about the Diet of Worms after all these years? The history mistress at school had never made it very clear what it had all been about, but then Miss Marlborough had always been the first to confess that religious controversies weren't her strong point. It obviously had nothing to do with proper worms, or proper diets for that matter. Wormelow: what a very odd name to give a child, as if it weren't bad enough to be saddled with a surname like Tump in the first place.

The poor man must have been teased about it a great deal as a child. Schoolboys could be very cruel . . . well, unthinking, really. Like all those people at the reception, so busy talking and wanting to be seen that none of them noticed how unwell Miss Naseby was looking. Still, once having grasped the point, Sir Wormelow had been kindness and efficiency itself. Who would ever have thought that Clive Bennett would one day have such distinguished friends!

Oh, dear, now comes the worst part. Miss Seeton gingerly disengaged first one foot from the opposite thigh, then the second, and with eyes closed, held her breath while the first wave of agony swamped her consciousness and then all too slowly receded. The pins and needles in all their glory were yet to come, but experience suggested that a period of total numbness and immobility would precede them, during which she might just as well turn her mind to other things.

Marigold Naseby, for example, or Susanna as she had thought of her since that day. Chaste Susanna. Delacroix? No, Chasseriau, of course. "Susanna and the Elders" . . . more than a little unfair to cast Clive in the role of an Elder, much less Sir Wormelow Tump; but theirs were the faces that lingered in the mind.

Tap, tap, tap . . . oh, dear, what a *very* embarrassing time for a visitor to call! Miss Seeton still had no sensation whatsoever in her legs, but she somehow contrived to drag herself to the window and peer out. Some feet below her stood the familiar figure of the vicar, who it was of course always a pleasure to see, even if one was at something of a disadvantage. . . .

"Good afternoon, Vicar!"

The Reverend Arthur Treeves looked up, his professional smile fading to be replaced by an expression of wonderment as he took in the spectacle of Miss Seeton's arms hanging limply over the windowsill, much as if she were an exhausted survivor of a shipwreck who had succeeded in reaching a lifeboat but lacked the strength to clamber in.

"Shall we have rain before the weekend, do you think?" the arms inquired politely, before to the vicar's great relief they were joined by Miss Seeton's head and neck.

"Ah, there you are. Good afternoon, Miss Seeton. Rain, you were saying? One cannot be sure, of course, but my sister thinks it very possible. She was indeed urging me over luncheon today to put the gardening tools I have been using recently back into the shed. Er . . . you are, I hope, quite well, Miss Seeton?"

"Indeed yes, thank you. I expect to be able to walk again quite soon."

"My dear lady, have you sustained an accident? Why

did not Mrs. Bloomer inform us?" Confused thoughts of beef tea and hot water bottles surged into Arthur Treeves's mind. Since realizing to his own surprise many years earlier that he had lost whatever faith he might once have possessed, the vicar had more or less come to terms with the situation. During their helpful little chat the bishop of Greenwich had urged him not to distress himself, explaining that a great many of the clergy and indeed not a few of his own brethren on the bench of bishops were in a very similar position, and that there was not the smallest evidence to suggest that this inhibited them in the performance of their duties.

The bishop was himself a go-ahead theologian, the author of several popular inspirational books whose titles tended to be expletives. *Strike a Light!* had done very well, and *For Heaven's Sake!* even better. Arthur Treeves envied the suffragan his breezy style, but no matter how often he was invited to do so simply could not bring himself to address him as "Rick." His advice had nonetheless been reassuring. "Just carry on in the normal way, my dear chap," the bishop had urged, "and you'll soon get used to it." And so he had, while still on the whole happier when doing good works than when conducting services.

"I shall ask my sister to call on you to see if there is any way in which—"

"No, no, Mr. Treeves, I assure you there is no need whatever for Miss Treeves to concern herself. In fact, I believe I can feel the pins and needles beginning now. The door is on the latch. Do please let yourself in. I shall be with you in no time at all, and we will have a nice cup of tea. I have been in the lotus posture, you see. I am told that Zen Buddhists can maintain it for hours without the least discomfort, but I daresay that is because they come to it earlier in life."

The vicar gazed at her in continuing bafflement for

some moments longer before shaking his head and doing as he had been bidden, standing uncertainly just inside the door to watch an otherwise cheery Miss Seeton totter down the stairs clinging to the banister rail. "Mind over matter, Vicar. That is what one must aim at, according to the manual. Do sit down, and I shall put the kettle on."

"Thank you. Yes, mind over matter. Quite so. I must say that for a moment I was most alarmed, but clearly all is well . . . though I understand you did in fact undergo a distressing experience a few days ago?"

"A distressing experience? Oh, you must mean the gentleman who was so badly scratched. His jacket was torn as well, I fear, and for a while he had great difficulty in breathing. No, quite the reverse, I assure you, Vicar," Miss Seeton said, now fully restored and bustling from the kitchen with several chocolate ginger biscuits on a plate. "It was he who was distressed. I was quite myself again within a few minutes, and indeed went on to enjoy a cup of coffee and a helpful chat with Lady Colveden."

The vicar blenched. This time it was true, then. Molly always insisted that Miss Nuttel and Mrs. Blaine not only invented things but persistently launched malicious rumors, particularly where Miss Seeton was concerned. There could, however, be no doubt that they had witnessed some sort of an incident in which she and an unknown man had been involved, an incident into which it seemed the police had deemed it necessary to inquire. And now here was Miss Seeton confirming the allegations made by the Nuts —oh, dear, it really was extremely uncharitable to refer to them so unkindly—by Miss Nuttel and Mrs. Blaine, when they had accosted him earlier that day.

Arthur Treeves was a bulky man who perspired freely in warm weather, and when embarrassed. The combination of the two sets of circumstances made it necessary for him to take out his handkerchief and dab first at his forehead, and then at the perfectly circular bald area on the top of his head that gave him such a convincingly clerical look. He cleared his throat nervously. He absolutely *hated* having to bring religion into conversations.

"Here in Plummergen we try, as you know, to avoid extremes of churchmanship," he began, falteringly. "And the preface to the Book of Common Prayer clearly implies that this is a wholly desirable course. On the other hand— and this is not perhaps as widely known as it should be— the sacrament of confession is always available to anyone in any parish who may have a troubled conscience. . . ."

"*You*, Mr. Treeves? A troubled conscience? I am sorry to hear it. It may be impertinent on my part to say so, but I am confident that you lead the most blameless of lives. I should of course be honored if you should wish to confide in me, but would not perhaps your sister be a more suitable—?"

"I fear I have expressed myself badly. What I . . . oh, never mind, Miss Seeton. Perhaps some other time." The vicar sighed and took refuge in his tea and the quite excellent biscuit. He had at least tried. Pastoral care, the bishop had stressed, had very little to do with theology or doctrine. One occasionally came across the odd eccentric who liked nothing better than a dingdong argument about transubstantiation; and of course people did get quite excited about the number of candles on the altar and so forth but could generally be calmed down without too much trouble. Coolly ruthless person she might now have revealed herself to be under that mild exterior, but at least Miss Seeton wasn't a religious maniac.

"Well, of course, if you say so," she went on after a moment, peering into the teapot to conceal her embarrassment over the vicar's unexpected cri de coeur. "I'm sure in any case whatever it is that may be worrying you will all look much less troublesome in the morning . . . Vicar!

You're just the person for me to ask! Now what *was* the Diet of Worms all about?"

Twenty minutes later, Miss Seeton, still much concerned, watched her dejected guest lurch away from Sweetbriars, head bowed and shoulders slumped. *Whatever* could Mr. Treeves have been up to? He had obviously been so completely distracted by whatever it was he had on his mind that he had shown no interest whatever in the Diet of Worms and, though it was hard to credit, seemed hardly even to have heard of Martin Luther. Or was it John Calvin?

Her musings were interrupted by the sound of the telephone ringing, and she hastened to answer it.

"Yes, this is Emily Seeton. I'm so sorry, I didn't quite catch . . . Who? Mel? Mel Forby? Why, Miss Forby, what an unexpected pleasure! Yes, of course I remember. You were so very kind to me when I was wet through. Though I do try not to think about those poor children. Thank you, yes, I am very well, except for being a little anxious about the vicar. Do *you* happen to know whether it was John Calvin or Martin Luther who had something to do with the Diet of Worms? You don't? Well, never mind. In Canterbury, you say? On holiday? How very nice, and not very far from here, of course. Why, that would be delightful, but if you have a car, why don't you come and have tea with me here at Sweetbriars, perhaps tomorrow? You will? Splendid! I shall look forward very much to seeing you again and telling you my exciting news. . . . "

chapter
~10~

"So I wouldn't want you to think there was anything, well, you know, out of order about what I did. Marigold Naseby —that's not her real name, by the way—"

"Oh, dear. Not Northamptonshire, then?"

"Northamptonshire? Sorry, I'm not with you."

"I was thinking of the Battle of Naseby, and assumed a family connection."

"Oh, I see. No, her family comes from Shepherd's Bush, I think. In London. Anyway, Marigold had a lot of help, sure, but there was nothing in the rules against that, and plenty of the other girls had smart professionals working on their images, too. I got nothing out of it except a lot of fun and the satisfaction of helping a clever photographer and good friend of mine to turn a nice but kind of ordinary kid into the Lalique Lady that Cedric Benbow freely chose. She won the contest fair and square."

Miss Seeton nodded immediately. "I'm quite sure she did, er, Mel." The modern fashion for using first names was so difficult to get used to, and though one must of course do as she asked, one would always want to think of her as Miss Forby. Amelita was the name she used professionally, of course, but that sounded even less right than Mel. Especially now that she made the best of those beautiful eyes of hers, and spoke in a more natural way. "And you will naturally be interested to know whether the photographs Mr. Benbow takes will please all concerned."

"I certainly will. And I wanted to be on hand in case the kid begins to buckle under pressure and needs support. But although as I've explained there was nothing whatever wrong about what I did, it still wouldn't look too good if it got out that I was, well, sort of her coach. That's why I decided not to stay here in Plummergen where a good many people know me. Canterbury's just half an hour away by car, so I can come running if need be, and I was wondering . . . well, what I mean is that you and the Colvedens are good friends, and you'd probably hear how things are going and might be kind enough to . . ."

"Of course I will," Miss Seeton said.

"That's great! Thanks a million. Anyway, that's quite enough about that. Now I want to hear more about this invitation from the Queen. What are you planning to wear?"

It had been decided that the most convenient place at Rytham Hall for Marigold Naseby to change in was the morning room on the ground floor, with the gowns and coats being stored on racks in Lady Colveden's small writing room, which opened off it. These two rooms therefore became almost exclusively the domain of Wendy and the indispensable Liz, who was to function as her dresser as well as taking care of her makeup during the sessions, after the hairdresser had performed his daily magic. It sounded relatively straightforward but soon turned into hard work, because by the end of the first day Cedric Benbow had imposed his idiosyncratic style on everybody.

"Feller's never heard of time and motion studies," Sir George commented affably enough to his son as Benbow flitted past the open door of the library yet again, pursued by his retinue of assistants carrying tripods and lighting equipment. After breakfast Lady Colveden had taken one look at the chaos in the hall, shuddered, and decided to drive into Brettenden, look at the shops, and have lunch there. Sir George on the other hand, as Nigel had predicted, was fascinated by everything and had only with some difficulty been dissuaded from offering to lend Benbow a hand.

"You'd think he'd get the gel tricked out in one of those frocks, then park her in one place, and finish one thing at a time, wouldn't you? Instead of firing off a few, then making her change, then change back into the first one again half an hour later. I must say I think those little silver umbrella things are rather neat. Didn't realize how many gadgets you need for a job like this. Might take up photography meself again one of these days." He turned to the large Securicor guard who was sitting to attention beside the locked strongbox in which the jewelry was kept. "You keen on it at all, Smithers? Photography."

Smithers had been a regular soldier for a good many years before joining Securicor and had, indeed, achieved the rank of corporal, but he had never previously been alone in the company of a major general, even a retired one. Sir George had within minutes winkled the details of his military career out of him and from then on treated the gratified Smithers as an old and valued comrade. All the same Smithers's muscles had been so conditioned by army life that they refused to relax, and he managed only a sort of gargling sound by way of reply.

"What's that you say? Expensive hobby? Absolutely. Couldn't agree more. Worth thinking about, though. Takes me back, you know, all this business today does, Nigel."

"What, *fashion* photography? Have you been hiding something from me, Dad?"

"Don't be a damn fool, boy, of course not. No, no. Manning the old command post, I mean. On the qui vive, eh, Smithers? Pickets mounted, alarm systems checked..."—he nodded toward the telephone—"and watches synchron—no, they aren't, dammit! Forgot about that." Sir George glanced at his own watch and registered surprise. "Heavens, nearly twenty past six; how time flies. My word, old Benbow keeps at it, don't he?"

"I think they are finishing for the day, actually, Dad. Er, if it's all right with you, I believe I'll just stroll down to the village with, er, Marigold. Um, I might get a bite to eat there, too. Tell Ma, would you?"

"By all means, by all means; all the more for us. Smithers and I will hold the fort. Have a bit of a yarn here till they bring—what is it, bracelet, couple of rings, and that huge brooch affair that looks like a stag beetle, right?"

"YesSAH!"

"Jolly good; at ease, old man. Yes, well, as soon as they bring that little lot back, we'll sign it off, march everything to the armored vehicle, and then fall out ourselves. Run the gel down to the pub in your car, I would, Nigel. Looks a bit seedy, if you ask me."

When Wendy and Liz emerged from the house ten minutes later, Nigel was leaning nonchalantly against the hood of his MG.

"Oh, gosh, it's you, Marigold!" he said in tones of delighted surprise, then, less enthusiastically, "and you, Liz. Went pretty well today, from what I could judge. You must be tired, though. Going back to the pub?"

Liz cheerfully declined the role of gooseberry. "Great! Here's the U.S. Cavalry. Got a job for you, Nige. I know that old banger of yours is only a two-seater, but Marigold's had a much 'arder day than me and I'd just as soon stretch me legs. Give her a lift; there's a duck."

"Oh, rather! I mean, absolutely, if you're sure it's okay by you, Liz."

Wendy protested, but feebly and not for very long, and was soon installed in the passenger seat. Liz grinned as Nigel started the little open car and gunned the engine impressively. "Take 'er the long way round, Romeo," she said. "This worryguts can do with a bit of fresh air and a change of company."

Wendy sat back, snugly held in the leather bucket seat, and let the mild evening breeze ruffle her hair. She *was* tired, knackered in fact, but it ought to have been happy tired. Everybody said Cedric was pleased with her. Mind you, he hadn't exactly said so himself. In fact, he was a right old fusspot. "No, darling, not like that, like *this*" —and then one of those killing two-second demonstrations when you forgot he was an old poof of about ninety with dyed hair and wished you could look half as classy as he did. And all that fiddling about for about half an hour till everything was ready and then: "No, this is going to be simply *dire*. Go and put the little magenta number on instead, poppet. And the silver pendant with the opals."

Bit different from the way Harry used to set about the job. Still, he had said she could call him Cedric, and patted her on the shoulder twice, and Liz said that was practically unheard of. So she ought to have been feeling really good now, bowling along in an MG and all. This Nigel bloke was a real upper-class twit in some ways, but all right really. Prob'ly couldn't help being wet, fancy having that old loony for a dad. The house was a bit of all right, though, and Liz said Nigel would be a Sir one day and that she thought he was definitely quite fanciable. What was the use of all that, though? Thursday, the phone man had said; oh, cripes, that was the day after tomorrow! Why didn't she just get this Nigel to drive them both off a cliff somewhere? What was the good of anything anymore?

"I say, Marigold, what about a drink? There's this rather nice pub I know just outside Brettenden: you can sit outside in the garden. Only about ten minutes from here."

"Don't mind."

"Terrific! Great!" Nigel had heard not a flat, sad little mutter but sheer poetry, accompanied by a glorious crescendo from massed stringed instruments. His own heart sang as he drove this miraculous creature along the least frequented lanes he could think of. Nobody, he vowed to himself, would ever be permitted to occupy that passenger seat again, not after it had been graced by Marigold's ethereal presence.

"Er, if you haven't got any other plans, you might like a bit of dinner there. It's quite good."

"Don't mind."

Nigel drove on, incapable of speech.

"All right, everybody, thank you; I think we can feel well pleased with this evening's work. What a difference it makes to be in costume, doesn't it? Final run-through next Tuesday, here at the same time, right?" Dr. Wright, who was himself dressed as a hippopotamus—for with his daughter, Anne, at the piano he sang "Mud, Mud, Glorious Mud" as well as directing the show—treated everybody in the cast to a cheery smile, and directed a specially warm one to his daughter and to her fiancé, Bob Ranger, who was present in a privileged-observer capacity since he might not be able to attend the actual performance. "Good night to you all!"

In the good-humored melee that followed in the George and Dragon's private dining room while people collected their belongings, the Reverend Arthur Treeves found himself in the company of the headmaster of the Plummergen village school.

"Went quite well, I thought, Vicar. Your 'Brown Boots' monologue was particularly good. Stanley Holloway to the life. And Potter was in excellent voice." Mr. Jessyp knew himself to possess a pleasing light tenor, and he warbled a bar or two of "A Policeman's Lot Is Not a Happy One," P. C. Potter's contribution to *Comical Capers*. This ambitious revue was to be given in the Brettenden Village Hall on the Saturday evening of the following week, in aid of the Plummergen Church Organ Fund. The vicar had therefore felt in duty bound to take an active part, much against his own inclinations.

"You are too modest, Mr. Jessyp. It is you and Mrs. Stillwell who will undoubtedly—what is the phrase?— 'stop the show.'" The headmaster, a slight man, was wearing plain dark blue trousers, a horizontally striped blue-and-white T-shirt with a jaunty red neckerchief and a blue beret, and his props consisted of a string of onions.

He had himself written the sketch in which he, as a French onion seller with a hilarious accent, simultaneously confused and misunderstood Mrs. Stillwell as a down-to-earth English housewife. The vicar was privately a little shocked by some of the double entendres in the dialogue and rather suspected it contained others he did not understand. In predicting huge success for the sketch, he was not being wholly sincere, but Mr. Jessyp accepted the tribute with a quiet, satisfied smile.

"We shall see, we shall see. Are you changing, Vicar? I came as I am, myself."

"I, too. It is no more than two or three minutes' walk from the vicarage, and fortunately I passed nobody on the

way. It is even less likely that anyone will be about so late
as a quarter to ten, with dusk upon us."

Mr. Jessyp concealed a smile, for like most amateur
actors he liked nothing better himself than to be seen in
costume by his acquaintances. He looked forward keenly
to plastering his face the following week with Leichner's
numbers five and nine greasepaint, and mingling with
members of the audience during the interval. Besides, the
vicar's costume was hardly outlandish, and his timidity
seemed excessive.

For his Stanley Holloway monologue Treeves's sister,
Molly, had decreed that if he were to dispense with his
clerical collar and its accompanying black dickey and leave
the top of his now collarless shirt open, his old gardening
clothes would suffice. A happy afterthought had made her
rummage through the attic and find a flat cap their father
had been wont to wear when he went to the races. This,
though a size too small for him, was now perched four-
square on the vicar's head.

"Shall we set off together, then? Our paths lie in the
same direction."

Wendy was feeling quite a lot better. She wasn't much
of a drinker, but the first gin and tonic of the evening had
given her an appetite, and the second made her inclined to
agree with Liz. If Nigel got rid of that crummy tweed
sports coat and bought some trendy gear, he wouldn't be
bad-looking at all. She hadn't expected the pub to have a
proper restaurant with tablecloths and a waitress and that,
and the look of awed amazement on the waitress's face
when she realized she was serving the famous Marigold
Naseby had cheered her up a treat, so much so that she'd
eaten all the whitebait Nigel ordered as a first course. It
was creepy eating them whole, little eyes and all, but if
you didn't look it wasn't too bad, and they tasted all right.

The fillet steak with new potatoes and garden peas was even better. Nigel seemed to have money to burn: lashed out *three quid* for a bottle of red wine just like that! Even offered her a liqueur to go with the chocolate mousse, but she'd been feeling a bit high by then and he hadn't gone on about it. Considering she'd hardly opened her mouth except to drink gin and tonic in the first half hour, he'd been really nice. Seemed happy enough to rabbit on about some college he went to, not that she'd listened really. Then they'd got on to Cedric Benbow and her winning the competition and that, which had got her going a bit, that and the wine, so she'd hardly noticed him holding her hand after the girl brought the coffee and asked for her autograph.

In the circs it would have been a bit chintzy to have kicked up a fuss on the way back when Nigel stopped the car in that little dead end and then sat there like a lemon, obviously wanting to snog. Quite honestly, she'd been feeling a bit randy herself by that time, pleasant change after spending the past few days scared to death, and it seemed only fair to lean over and give him a big smoochy kiss. Then he gave her one back and they swapped a few more, quite on-turning but awkward in that titchy car. Just as well he hadn't suggested getting out—she might have got sort of carried away.

Anyway, it was nice just sitting there now, parked about a hundred yards away from the George and Dragon, on the other side of the road. Nigel wasn't trying anything, just holding her hand and kissing her fingers now and then in a dreamy sort of way, quite romantic really with it beginning to get dark.

Nigel himself wished time could stand still. It didn't matter that they were in full view of passersby. Nobody could enter their space, the cocoon of bliss in which he was floating with Marigold, whom he now dared to begin to think of as *his* Marigold. He squeezed her hand gently and was thrilled when she responded, her fingers gripping his. Then, however, her grasp took on an extraordinary, unnatural ferocity, and she began to utter a low, shuddering moan that gradually increased in volume until she herself clapped her free hand over her mouth and suppressed it, making instead a continuous series of muffled yelps, like a puppy shut in a cupboard.

"Marigold! Darling, whatever's the matter?" Nigel gazed at her in alarm, noticed that her eyes were bulging and that she was staring fixedly in the direction of the George and Dragon, and himself looked toward it. He could see nothing whatever to account for Marigold's behavior, just the vicar and Mr. Jessyp emerging from the door of the pub in the gathering gloom and crossing the road before turning toward them.

"It's *them*! Uncle Geor-or-*orge*! An' ArArALFIE! Don't let them see me; oh, *Gawd*, don't let them see me!" Wendy babbled before burying her face in Nigel's chest and clinging to him, shuddering.

chapter
~11~

"No, YOU did *quite* the right thing, Nigel," Miss Seeton insisted again, firmly ushering him toward the door. "As you can see, Miss Naseby is already feeling a great deal more composed, and she is enjoying her cocoa. She will be perfectly safe here with me tonight; the spare room is quite comfortable, if I say so myself, and I shall have her bed made up in a jiffy. And Miss Naseby won't be nervous because nobody but we three have the slightest idea where she is, isn't that so? And I'm sure she can trust you implicitly."

"Oh, yes, *yes*," Nigel groaned fervently. "You can, Marigold, you can. But if only there were some way I could persuade you . . ." It was clear to Miss Seeton that she had only to say the word and he would willingly keep a vigil all night outside the cottage, but that would never do.

"Telephone me as early as you like in the morning, Nigel, and you will be the first to know whether Miss Naseby feels able to work tomorrow. I'm quite sure she will, you know. Good night!"

After many another wild-eyed, adoring glance at his be-loved, who was sitting on Miss Seeton's sofa with one of her shawls round her shoulders and clutching her mug of cocoa, Nigel was finally persuaded to go.

Miss Seeton closed the door behind him with a sigh of relief and locked it. Nigel was a very fine young man in so many ways, but oh, dear, how he had badgered the poor girl with incomprehensible and surely irrelevant questions about her relatives! It was enough, surely, that something had frightened her very badly and that she adamantly—in-deed almost hysterically—insisted that nothing would make her set foot in the George and Dragon, now that *they*, whoever *they* might be, had tracked her down.

What the child needed was a good night's sleep and one, or perhaps even two, of Stan Bloomer's free-range eggs in the morning. It was of no use at all when she was in such a highly nervous state to try to persuade her that she had been imagining things, much less to ask really quite impertinent things about her family. That was com-pletely out of order. The thing to do was to go and sit quietly beside her, perhaps pat her hand gently—after she had finished her cocoa, of course; otherwise she might spill it—and talk about something quite different until she had calmed down. Then get her tucked up in bed.

Wendy was still producing occasional lurching sobs when Miss Seeton joined her on the sofa, but managed a timid smile even so.

"I 'spect you think I'm bonkers, too, like Nige does."

"Good gracious, no! My dear girl, I've been concerned about you ever since I saw you at the gallery in London. Now do tell me, why should the thought of your Uncle George upset you so much?"

"He's not really her uncle at all, you see, Mr. Ranger. And nor is the other man, whose name is Alfie, any kind of cousin, it seems. They may or may not be related to the telephone man, but I'm not entirely clear about that."

Bob Ranger removed the receiver from his ear and gazed at it for a moment uncomprehendingly before replacing it. "The telephone man, Miss Seeton?"

"Yes. Or possibly the Slicer."

"The Slicer. What sort of slicer would that be? A bacon slicer?"

"No, not that kind of slicer; a person. A friend of the telephone man. He was very disappointed in his wife, and with good reason, I gather. But not, of course, enough to justify his disgraceful behavior."

Bob Ranger was sitting in the study of Dr. Wright's large house, to which the doctor's private nursing home and clinic were annexed. Since becoming engaged to Anne, he was always warmly welcomed by all three Wrights as an overnight guest, most of all by his fiancée. Anne was indeed at that moment perched on Bob's lap, but had tactfully stopped nibbling at his right earlobe when she realized who was on the other end of the line.

"I see. That is, I'm afraid I don't understand. I think I'd better pop along to your house, Miss Seeton." He looked at his watch: it was just after eleven-fifteen. "Unless it's too late for you?"

"A very kind thought, but I'm afraid if you were to come now, it would upset Miss Naseby all over again, just when she's settled down nicely. She would assume you were the Slicer, you see."

"Ah. Well, I wouldn't want her to think that."

"Dear me, no. I ventured to telephone simply to let you know she's here with me, and quite safe, but I do think it would be helpful if you could possibly spare a few minutes in the morning. Poor child, when it all began to come out it was so like the story of Susanna and the Elders, just as I had imagined. I'm sure that by breakfast time I shall have persuaded her to tell you all about it. And if necessary I shall speak to Mr. Benbow myself. Quite firmly. There must be no nonsense about his engaging the services of a different model."

"Absolutely not, Miss Seeton," said Bob, utterly lost.

"I'm afraid that before I persuaded him to leave us together, Nigel Colveden confused the issue a great deal, trying to convince her it was Mr. Treeves who had frightened her."

"The vicar? Why on earth should he want to frighten Marigold Naseby?"

"I really couldn't say. He's very well-meaning and of course hopelessly infatuated with her."

"I'm sorry, Miss Seeton, but I find that very hard to believe. He's certainly well-meaning—one more or less takes that for granted in a vicar—but—"

"Not the vicar, Mr. Ranger, Nigel." A lengthy silence followed before Bob came to a decision and spoke again.

"I see. Yes. Well, it's extremely good of you to report all this, Miss Seeton, and I'll be glad to drop in first thing in the morning to have a word with the young lady, if that'll suit you. Eight o'clock too early? Fine. Good night, then."

As he put the receiver down, Anne gazed up at him. "I love you when you go all cross-eyed like that," she said, and then busied herself with his ear again.

Just over three hours later, some thirty miles away in Sussex Sir Sebastian Prothero slithered noiselessly out of the kitchen window at Melbury Manor and gestured airily toward the darkened house, slipped the knapsack off his shoulders, and swung it casually in his hand as he made his way back to his car.

It had been a doddle, and to think he'd nearly decided to let it go, to save himself for the Rytham Hall job! No, there's a tide in the affairs of men, he vaguely remembered somebody or other pointing out in one of his school textbooks, and when you realize it's coming your way the thing is to get out the old water wings, lie back, and enjoy it. A gift from the gods, pure and simple—old Carfax the property tycoon coming into the Club Mondial that evening with his glamorous new wife.

Fancy blithering on like that! About having planned to go down to Sussex but having to stay in town for the rest of the week because the resident housekeeper who took care of Melbury Manor had been in dock having her varicose veins sorted out. And now she and her husband, the butler/handyman, were off in Runcorn, or some such ghastly place, staying with their married daughter. And obviously Sandra could hardly be expected to... well, old Carfax was right about that at least. The new Mrs. Carfax was obviously good at things not associated with housework, and judging by the way she'd been giving him sidelong glances, wouldn't, within a few months, mind demonstrating her skills to Sir Sebastian.

Be that as it may, there were the Carfaxes tucked up in Claridges Hotel in London and their resident Sussex servitors ditto in Runcorn. While he, Sebastian Prothero, was tooling back to London with his knapsack. This now contained not only his surgical rubber gloves, the white cotton ones he wore over them, and the simple kit of tools experience had led him to put together, but also a pair of rather nice miniatures in ornate silver frames, an elegant little ormolu clock, and a very nice diamond bracelet Sandra had foolishly left in the drawer of her bedside table. If the clock had been just a shade bigger, Prothero would have left it behind, for portability was one of his main criteria of selection. It was a pretty thing, though, and he might even take the risk of hanging on to it for himself.

Ah, good, there was a twenty-four-hour Esso station

just ahead. Setting off on the spur of the moment full of adrenaline like that, he hadn't thought to check the gas gauge until after the job was over. As he was getting back into the car after filling the tank and paying, it occurred to him that there wasn't much point in returning to London anyway. He was still much too elated to sleep. It was already Wednesday and he'd always intended to go down to Kent then, to have a last-minute look around before the big effort. Why not go straight across country, enjoy the dawning of another fine summer day? Why not?

When Prothero drove out of the filling station, he headed not for London but more or less due east, on a course that would take him through Tunbridge Wells and then in the direction of Canterbury. He thought Canterbury would be a good place to put up: in the general vicinity of Plummergen but far enough away to avoid the likelihood of accidental encounters with anybody involved in the Cedric Benbow circus. Full of tourists at this time of the year, too: excellent cover. He always kept an overnight bag in his car—and had often been glad of it while greeting the morning in a succession of new lady friends' bathrooms—and a selection of clean clothes, so that would be no problem.

Sir Sebastian never claimed to be musical, but he hummed a snatch of "This Is My Lucky Day" to himself. A spot of ultraearly breakfast first to settle his stomach, at some all-night transport café where his unshaven face, dark sweater, slacks, and rubber-soled canvas shoes would arouse no curiosity: that would be the thing. Then find a lay-by in a quiet country road and stretch out in the car for a bit of ziz before running his battery-powered shaver over his face.

After that, change out of his working clothes and into something suitable for Canterbury and off we go. Via Plummergen, maybe! What a marvelous piece of cheek it would be to find a public telephone box on the outskirts of the village itself from which to ring Marigold Naseby at the George and Dragon! A morning call, just to make sure she was still properly cowed and ready to do her bit on Thursday as instructed. Yes, that would be an elegantly audacious thing to do.

Meantime, it might be wise to put some more miles between him and Melbury Manor. The adrenaline still coursing through his body, Prothero slipped from third into top gear, and twiddled the dial of the car radio to see if he could find some music to match his elated mood.

chapter
~12~

WHEN BOB Ranger arrived at Sweetbriars punctually at eight the following morning, it was to find a council of war already in session round the kitchen table, with Martha Bloomer in the capacity of supplies officer refilling coffee cups and urging more toast on the participants. These comprised not only Miss Seeton and a Marigold Naseby who looked simultaneously bewildered and relieved, but also Cedric Benbow, natty in white linen trousers and a garment resembling a sailor's blouse except that it was pale blue. The ensemble gave him a delicately nautical air. At the head of the table was Sir George Colveden, the picture of ruddy good humor.

"Ah, there you are, Ranger! Well done; take a pew," Sir George said genially. There was no possible doubt who was in charge. "Introductions in order, what? Miss Seeton's already explained who you are, of course. Miss Naseby, allow me to present Detective Sergeant Ranger of Scotland Yard. Miss Marigold Naseby. Benbow old boy, this is Bob Ranger. Mr. Cedric Benbow, the distinguished photographer. He's very sportingly offered to show me round his studio sometime." He lowered his voice. "My son, Nigel, was here, but the boy was dithering. Embarrassing Miss Naseby and getting in everybody's way. Sent him over to the George and Dragon to tell the others they don't need to get up to the Hall before o-nine thirty hours after all. Spot of coffee? I'm sure the good Mrs. Bloomer here . . ." He went even redder in the face and subsided, belatedly remembering where he was. Bob nodded greeting to Benbow and Wendy, and Miss Seeton was enabled to get a word in.

"Have you breakfasted, Mr. Ranger?"

"Thank you, yes. A cup of coffee would be very welcome, though. Thanks, Mrs. Bloomer. No, no toast, thanks."

"I fear that events have somewhat overtaken us, Mr. Ranger."

"My fault, Sergeant," Benbow put in. "I was up and about very early and decided to try to catch the light. Rang the pub to get people up to the house right away. Ten minutes later my chap rang back to say they couldn't find Marigold. Nigel Colveden took the call."

Sir George had recovered his self-possession. "Blithering idiot didn't know what to do for the best. I was up and about by then, giving the dogs their Chummy Chunks, you know—they prefer me to do it. Experienced interrogator, soon got it out of the lad that the gel, I beg your pardon, m'dear, Miss Naseby, was here at Miss Seeton's—"

"And Mr. Benbow telephoned me," Miss Seeton gently but firmly interjected. "He and I are very old acquaintances, you see, and in view of what Miss Naseby had told me last night I was very pleased to have an opportunity for a private word with him. It would have been difficult to fit it in later, because Lady Colveden is very kindly coming for me at nine-thirty, so that we can both have our hair done in Brettenden. For the garden party, you know. At Buckingham Palace."

"Confoundedly awkward it's today, Ranger. Needed here really, but there you are. Hire car coming to fetch the three of us at noon. Got to allow a good couple of hours to get there, plus time for the mems to pop into that hotel at Victoria Station to titivate themselves."

Bob felt himself going down for the third time and realized that stern measures were called for. He cleared his throat noisily and then took a deep breath, which had the effect of making him look even more huge and reduced everybody momentarily to silence. He then smiled encouragingly at Wendy. "And what, Miss Naseby, did you tell Miss Seeton last night?"

The tapping on the car window was gentle but insistent, and it annoyed Prothero as he struggled up through the mists of sleep. Then, still only half-awake, he remembered where he was. On the edge of Plummergen, in a lane that seemed to lead nowhere in particular and had, in the small hours, struck him as an ideal place to park for the snooze he very definitely needed after the huge fry-up he had eaten in the all-night transport café. The realization jolted him into full consciousness and made him sit bolt upright in the seat he had tipped back for greater comfort.

For a moment he thought he must still be asleep and dreaming, then devoutly wished he was. For the tapping at the window was the work of the mad old bat who had assaulted him near Rytham Hall and who had very nearly caught his eye outside the Szabo Gallery. Now she was nodding and beaming at him in the friendliest way, and miming the action of drinking a cup of tea. Briefly tempted to start the engine and make an unceremonious getaway, Prothero thought better of it. That would more than likely do more harm than good. Better try to bluff his way out of trouble again. With a sinking feeling he wound the window down.

"I expect you dropped off after listening to the dawn chorus," Miss Seeton said. "I do hope I'm not disturbing you, but I saw your car from my bedroom window, you see, and recognized it. So since it's nearly nine o'clock, I thought I'd come and ask you if you would care for a cup of tea or coffee. The others have all just gone off to Rytham Hall, and there's lots left. Of coffee, that is, though it would be no trouble to make you some tea if you would prefer it. I know you won't mind if I go on getting ready, but Lady Colveden is very kindly coming for me in half an hour. She insists that we must look our best for Buckingham Palace, you see."

Prothero thought quickly. Crazy she undoubtedly was, going on about Buckingham Palace, but nevertheless her references to Rytham Hall and Lady Colveden were worrying. And she had been at the gallery, after all. Better go along with her and find out just what the connection was. Ought not to be difficult, the way she went on about herself. With an effort he turned on the charm and got out of the car.

"How very kind of you. I do apologize for my appearance. My clothes, I mean, and not having shaved."

"Not at all. I can well imagine that enthusiastic birdwatchers must be up at all hours. What a coincidence that you should have parked your car so near my cottage."

"No, I didn't even begin to make any sense of it all until much later, sir. It was like the Mad Hatter's tea party there. The girl had obviously reached the point where she was only too ready to spill the beans, but Sir George kept warning her off. Muttering 'no names, no pack drill, m'dear' and winking in the direction of Miss Seeton's cleaning lady. Between them they were sending me up the wall."

"I can well imagine it," Delphick said, heaving with suppressed mirth at the other end of the line as he visualized the scene. "But you say you began to make sense of it later. Tell me more."

"Yes, sir. Well, before I got there it seems Miss Seeton and Cedric Benbow had already persuaded the girl not to quit, and to go to Rytham Hall for the day's session as planned. So since we obviously weren't getting anywhere round Miss Seeton's kitchen table, I suggested we should adjourn. It was quite a cavalcade. Nigel Colveden was very put out when Benbow insisted Marigold Naseby should ride with him in Sir George's car rather than in Nigel's MG. Nigel got stuck with me."

"If it was that little two-seater of his, I'm surprised it wasn't you who got stuck, Bob."

"Mm. Was the dickens of a squeeze, I must admit, and it wasn't as if I got anything useful out of him. He kept raving about the vicar for some reason. Miss S. must have been glad to see the back of us. By the way, sir, did you know she's at a garden party at Buckingham Palace this afternoon?"

"Miss Seeton? Good heavens. No, I had no idea. Her Majesty's advisers must be out of their minds."

"With Sir George and Lady Colveden. Quite frankly, sir, it's a great relief to have them out of the way for the rest of the day. Miss Seeton went off with Lady C. to have her hair done, but the general was very much in charge at the Hall for another couple of hours until he had to go upstairs and get into his morning suit. Up till then he'd been prowling about with the Securicor man in tow, going on about booby traps and perimeter tripwires. Not much I could do: he's a JP and it is his house, after all. Sir, I think all the Colvedens are probably mad."

"No, no. Perfectly normal upper-class behavior, I'd say. Meantime Benbow was snapping away cheerfully enough, was he?"

"Yes. It's astonishing, he and Sir George seem to be getting along together famously. And Marigold Naseby had cheered up a lot, so everything was moving along according to plan, except that I was left twiddling my thumbs, still completely in the dark. Until a hire car turned up just before twelve noon and Sir George and Lady Colveden pushed off in it to pick up Miss S. and go to London. The moment they disappeared down the drive, Cedric Benbow sent his assistant to find me, then called a break, and took me for a walk in the grounds. Sorry to take so long explaining all this, sir."

"Don't apologize. I'm all ears."

"So was I. All that flouncing around and darling this and darling that's just for show, sir. Basically, Benbow's a very straightforward chap, sharp as a tack. Explained the situation in plain English in about six sentences. The girl's being blackmailed. Before she made her name by winning the competition she was just a small-time, more or less amateur model. She posed for a set of pin-up pictures that were never used, but the villain's got hold of them somehow. His price for not selling them to one of the sleazy papers is that she should nick some of the Lalique jewelry for him."

"How? I thought it was supposed to be under guard night and day."

"He's got it all worked out. Marigold's the only person who could possibly arrange to be alone with any of it, by pretending to be taken short while she's wearing it, and rushing to the bathroom. There she's to chuck it out of the window into his waiting hands, and stagger out a few minutes later white-faced with a tale of a masked man lurking inside and relieving her of it at the point of a knife."

"Good grief, nobody would believe a tale like that for a second, Bob!"

"Of course not, sir. She'd be nabbed on sus right away and eventually done as an accessory, but she doesn't realize that. The blackmailer does, of course. He's not a nice man. He's quite ruthlessly planning to throw her to the wolves. It wouldn't matter a hoot to him what she said after being arrested, because she hasn't the faintest idea who he is. I'm looking forward to getting my hands on him," Bob added thoughtfully, and Delphick involuntarily shuddered.

"You've told Mr. Brinton in Ashford all this, presumably?"

"Yes, sir, before I rang you. Hope that was the right thing."

"Of course. You're down there to help him, not me. I imagine he isn't too pleased that so many people know about all this."

"The main problem, sir, is that so many people know about all this," Chief Inspector Brinton said to his chief constable. "Apart from us and Scotland Yard, I mean."

"Who does, precisely?"

"Precisely? Rather hard to say, sir. The young woman, of course, though she's been spared having the implications spelled out to her. The mess she could have found herself in if she'd kept it to herself, I mean. Then there's Miss Seeton, who persuaded her to open up. Cedric Benbow, and Major General Colveden."

"Oh, Lord. George Colveden isn't a man to keep a secret."

"I'd have to agree with you there, sir. But he's out of harm's way at least until tomorrow, when with a bit of luck we shall have chummy in the bag. He and Lady Colveden, plus Miss Seeton, incidentally, are all at the Queen's garden party this afternoon. Won't be back until after Ben-

bow's finished his photography for the day. Miss Seeton
will keep mum, I'm sure. And even if she were to let
something slip by accident, knowing her, I doubt if anybody would have the vaguest idea what she was talking
about."

"If you say so, Brinton. I may give George Colveden a
ring myself this evening, warn him to keep his trap shut.
This photographer chap, Benbow. He's sound, you say?"

"I haven't spoken to him myself yet, sir, but he seems
to have impressed Sergeant Ranger, and I set a lot of store
by Ranger's judgment. He says Benbow's clear-thinking,
decisive, and practical. It seems he sorted the girl out in no
time by making it clear that come what may, he has no
intention of ditching her from this Lalique job. Ranger's
sure he won't give the game away."

"Fair enough. Sounds a decent sort of chap. Now I
know you think I'm an interfering old buffer, Brinton—"

"Not at all, sir—"

"Oh, yes, you do, but if you're going to deny it try a bit
harder to sound convincing, would you? Anyway, be that
as it may, what I was about to say was this: I can't believe
that covers everybody. Surely there must be all sorts of
gossip flying around by now? You know what those village
people are like."

"Gossip, certainly, but most of it well off the mark. Let
me give you an example. A Miss Nuttel—you probably
won't know of her, sir, but she and the woman she shares a
house with, Mrs. Blaine, been thorns in our side for years,
the pair of 'em. Wicked tongues and wild imaginations
they have. Well, this Miss Nuttel rang the village copper,
P. C. Potter, to report that Nigel Colveden had abducted a
young woman and handed her over in a terrible state to
Miss Seeton, who is, among a lot of other things according

to her, almost certainly a white-slaver who plans to ship the girl off to Buenos Aires."

"Buenos Aires? What on earth for? There are plenty of white-slave outlets in London. In Maidstone and Tunbridge Wells, too, I shouldn't wonder."

"Quite, sir. Figure of speech, I shouldn't wonder."

"No doubt. Young Colveden must be involved some-how, though. You mentioned him earlier. So presumably he must be another one who's got to be shut up."

"Not really necessary, sir. He doesn't know anything about the pinup photos or the blackmail. He seems to be under the impression that the girl is terrified of her uncle and a cousin or something. He claims she saw the vicar of Plummergen and the headmaster of the village school com-ing out of the George and Dragon, where she was staying, and mistook them for her relatives. Jumped to the conclu-sion that they were after her and got into such a state that young Colveden thought he'd better take her to Miss See-ton's place."

"Extraordinary sort of mistake to make, surely?"

"In fairness to her it does appear that the blackmailer—who has only ever been in touch with her by phone—did also threaten to hire thugs to beat her up if she didn't play ball. Nigel Colveden's got hold of the wrong end of the stick entirely, though."

"Ha! Not unlike his father. Though I must admit Colve-den senior's a pretty wily old bird when all's said and done. Well, what do you propose to do about all this, Brin-ton?"

"Well, to put it at its simplest, set an ambush and nab him, sir. Preferably red-handed. We're convinced he's the mystery man Miss Seeton saw snooping around near Rytham Hall some while ago. And thanks to a remarkable likeness she produced—and to some good thinking on the part of P. C. Potter—we're pretty sure the same chap managed to con his way into the house last week and have a good look round."

"But you don't know who he is."

"Not a clue I'm afraid, sir. Drawn a blank there. Soon find out after we catch him, though."

Sir Sebastian Prothero registered at the White Swan in Canterbury under the name of his useful acquaintance the gossip columnist. It wasn't much after eleven-thirty, but he gazed soulfully at the receptionist and she, recognizing the name, decided on the spot that hc could have the use of his room at once rather than having to wait until check-in time at two.

The loot from Melbury Manor he'd left locked in the trunk of his car. Both the Automobile Association and the Royal Automobile Club judged the White Swan to be worthy of three stars, though its parking lot was small. So much the better from Prothero's point of view, because it meant that it was strictly reserved for registered guests only, and jealously watched over by an attendant, whose day Prothero made by giving him a pound.

The stuff would as a result be perfectly safe where it was, particularly since the lock on the trunk was not that originally provided by the manufacturers of the car but an ingenious and expensive replacement claimed by its makers to be burglar-proof. Prothero was a great believer in doing everything possible to protect his possessions, though pleased of course that so few people seemed to be as careful as he.

The bathwater was hot, and he soaked himself in it for a long time, going over and over every aspect of the situation, not wanting to face the fact that he was going to have to do something about Miss Seeton. It was an important part of Prothero's job to read the popular papers, and it had come as a very nasty shock when she introduced herself to realize that he was tangling with the famous Battling Brolly in person. It had been a hell of an effort to sit there in her cottage, drink her coffee, and make polite conversation with the knowledge that she was well in with the police, no matter how dotty she came across.

It had not been until afterward, on the way to Canterbury, that the possibility of murdering her had occurred to him, to be dismissed at once as being out of the question. He was a master criminal, certainly, but no murderer. A soldier of fortune, a stylish burglar, not a killer. But the insidious idea kept coming back, in subtly different ways. Not a killer? Think again. The former Captain Prothero of the Guards was, like most professional soldiers, a *trained* killer. And we all have to die sometime. Miss Seeton was elderly. Not at all that many years to go in any case. Above all, she was dangerous, because if she was as smart as the papers claimed, and Scotland Yard thought so much of her, she might have been capable of setting up that little chat on purpose.

Above all, and whether or not she was already on to him, she was in a position to identify him as having been in the vicinity of Rytham Hall in suspicious circumstances the previous week. Just when everything had been going so well, confound it, and he had been in complete command of the situation, with a perfect set-up!

That stupid little Naseby trollop was in a state of gibbering terror and positively eager to follow his instructions to the letter the next day. While Benbow's people would all be dancing attendance on the ridiculous old queen, needless to say. He could therefore take his time over getting into position in the excellent cover provided by the shrubbery no more than a few yards away, and by the time any sort of hue and cry was raised he, Sir Sebastian Prothero, would be elsewhere. And in any case they wouldn't be looking for him. In time they might be looking for a voice on the phone, perhaps, and the best of British luck to them.

If, and only if, he first disposed of the Seeton woman.

He hauled himself up out of the water and reached for the bath towel. It would have to be done that night.

chapter
~13~

DEPUTY ASSISTANT Commissioner Roland Fenn had not originally planned to go personally to the Queen's garden party, but in the end simple curiosity got the better of him. As head of the Special Branch he needed no invitation, but it was necessary for him to fit in a quick visit to Moss Bros. in Covent Garden and rent the appropriate clothes; and he had done this during the previous afternoon.

Now, resplendent in morning suit, gray waistcoat, and silvery necktie, a topper perched jauntily on his well-groomed head, he strolled down Buckingham Gate in the direction of the Palace, basking in what he took for granted to be the admiring glances of passersby in ordinary clothes. It was, after all, no more than five minutes walk from New Scotland Yard. Each guest invited to a large-scale event such as a garden party was, he knew, provided with a card indicating which of several entrances to the Palace grounds he or she should use. Carrying the sort of credentials he did, Fenn could perfectly well have gone in through the main gates, but prompted by a desire to slip into the action as unobtrusively as possible, he turned into Buckingham Palace Road, crossed it, and made his way along the high boundary wall beyond the Royal Mews to the Grosvenor Place entrance.

There half a dozen or so obvious garden party guests were waiting patiently enough to hand over their admission cards to one of the two uniformed policemen who were scrutinizing each one, while an immensely tall, red-jacketed Coldstream guardsman loftily surveyed the scene from beneath his bearskin.

It was a pleasant sight, Fenn thought to himself. Once more Her Majesty's soothsayers had managed to arrange marvelous weather: or perhaps they had deliberately recommended a day during Wimbledon fortnight, which was invariably fine. The white-gloved ladies looked very charming in their summery silk dresses. So agreeable to see them all wearing hats, as well, in these all-too-informal times. And all the men, save one, morning-suited like himself. The exception was a very large black bishop in a splendid cassock. Of a hue closer to shocking pink than episcopal purple, it nevertheless suited him admirably, Fenn thought, and then became aware that a problem seemed to have arisen at the gate.

No doubt suitably awed by the occasion, those waiting to get in were much too polite to say anything; but a certain amount of foot-shuffling and a number of disapproving glances accompanied Fenn as he sidled round the group. This was becoming larger as newcomers joined it, while, it appeared, nobody was being admitted. Once he could properly see what was going on inside the gate, the reason for the disturbance was revealed to him in the form of a choleric gentleman accompanied by a lady who was evidently his wife, because she looked both cross and embarrassed and was tugging at his sleeve. The gentleman was for some reason berating one of the policemen on behalf of—yes, it had to be, it *could* only be Miss Seeton, who was standing meekly by.

There was no time to be lost. Fenn pushed his way through, ignoring the guardsman who took a menacing step forward, and after whispering into the ear of the second policeman, drew him aside. His back to the crowd outside the gate, Fenn quickly showed him his deputy assistant commissioner's warrant card. The policeman gulped and stiffened to attention. "What the devil's going on, Constable?" Fenn demanded.

"The gent and his wife are okay, sir. Lady with them, the one with the umbrella, she's supposed to go in a different gate. Got the wrong card for this one. Gent's objecting."

"So I should damn well think. They're together. I know who the lady is, and I'll personally vouch for her. Now tell your partner to stop messing about and let the three of them in at once."

Fenn didn't want to be identified as their savior by the couple he now knew to be the Colvedens, nor for that matter by Miss Seeton. He recognized her because he had been present in the background in Delphick's office during one of the occasional visits to Scotland Yard the Oracle asked her to make when he wanted to pump her. They hadn't been introduced, though, and he thought it most unlikely she would remember him, especially dressed as he was now. He therefore went straight through to the gardens and put a number of other people behind him before glancing back to make sure his instructions had been obeyed.

They had. Sir George, Lady Colveden, and Miss Seeton were in plain view. Sir George still looked a little heated and was gesticulating vigorously to Miss Seeton, but Lady Colveden must already have spotted an acquaintance. She was in conversation with an aged lady the hem of whose dress had become partially detached and whose hat had a

distinctly prewar look to it. Splendid. As Fenn watched,
Lady Colveden turned and was obviously summoning her
husband to heel, while Miss Seeton was equally clearly
seizing the opportunity to detach herself from her protector
and champion.

Once free she looked about her with what even from a
distance Fenn could see was an expression of mild relief.
Then she set off along a minor pathway, pausing from time
to time to stoop and inspect the herbaceous border. After a
suitable interval Fenn wandered in her wake, only too
pleased to have an opportunity to study her behavior at
leisure. He was also interested to see how long it would
take the Special Branch inspector detailed to engineer her
meeting with Wormelow Tump to locate and identify her.

"Pom, pom, pom," Miss Seeton murmured happily to
herself. Then, a little later, "Tiddle *pom*." She cocked her
head to catch more distinctly the sound of the band in the
distance. *The Yeomen of the Guard*, perhaps? Or was it
H.M.S. Pinafore? One could so easily become muddled
about which Savoy opera was which. It was so agreeable to
be on one's own for a short time, though one mustn't stray
too far. Sir George had been very insistent on that point,
and in any case it would be hardly polite to desert one's
hosts for long. Well, hosts only in a manner of speaking,
that is. One was in fact the guest of Her Majesty, even if,
as Lady Colveden had stressed, it was most unlikely one
would catch more than a glimpse of her.

Nevertheless, the Colvedens were so kind and generous.
It had perhaps not been necessary for Sir George to speak
quite so loudly at the entrance, but army officers did need
to make themselves heard on parade of course, and no
doubt found it difficult to reduce the volume after retire-
ment. One would have been perfectly happy to go to the
proper entrance alone; the one the police officer had

pointed out so clearly on the little map provided with the admission cards. So very clearly, and repeatedly. Yet somehow Sir George had prevailed, and when the policemen—who after all had their instructions—had eventually changed their minds and let them all in together, how very quickly it had all happened! And clearly it was quite in order to carry an umbrella, which no doubt counted as a parasol.

So now one was actually walking in the Queen's garden! Such a privilege, and such very beautiful flowers everywhere! The lawns alone were a picture, and there was the lake, and over there an enormous open-sided marquee, and the back of the Palace itself, peacefully dominating the scene. And an exquisitely beautiful butterfly down there among the flowers. Miss Seeton stopped abruptly, tucked her umbrella under her arm, and bent down for a closer look. Then, hearing a stifled yelp behind her, she looked up over her shoulder to see a young gentleman in morning dress gazing at her with an expression of agonized reproach while clutching at the front of his trousers.

"Oh, dear! I do beg your pardon. How very clumsy of me."

Inspector Adrian Harlow closed his watering eyes briefly, swaying on his feet, and then with a huge effort of will managed to pull himself together and adopt a more seemly posture.

"Perfectly all right, madam." To his alarm he heard a strangled squawk instead of the normally mellow baritone speaking voice on which he prided himself, cleared his throat, and tried again. "No damage done, I assure you." Better, thank heavens, but it had been a near thing. What he had heard was true, then: the old girl was a terror with that confounded brolly of hers. Think positively, Harlow. Try to look on the bright side. At least he'd identified her; as usual there were some pretty dotty-looking old trout doddering about the grounds, but surely there couldn't be another who matched so perfectly the description and photograph he'd been given. Better make sure, all the same.

"No problem at all. Perhaps I should introduce myself, though. Harlow, Adrian Harlow."

"Good afternoon, Mr. Harlow. My name is Emily Seeton. Miss. I am greatly relieved. It was nevertheless extremely thoughtless of me. It was the butterfly that caught my eye, you see, that and trying to decide between *The Yeomen of the Guard* and *H.M.S. Pinafore*. Or could it be *The Gondoliers*? That the band are playing?"

"I think it's something from *South Pacific*, actually, Miss Seeton." The pain had almost gone, and it was possible to think more or less clearly. "Have you been to one of these garden parties before?"

"Dear me, no. Indeed I am still at a loss to imagine why I should have been so honored."

"I'm sure you do yourself an injustice. I envy you: I should explain that I'm not actually a guest myself; I'm a member of the Palace staff. Um, sort of public relations, you might say. Introducing people, that sort of thing. If it would interest you, I'd be happy to point out one or two of the well-known people here today."

"How very kind of you, Mr. Harl . . ." Miss Seeton paused in embarrassment, it having all at once occurred to her that she was in the company of some sort of courtier who might easily have a title. "That is to say, I do hope I am correct in addressing you as mister?"

"Oh, absolutely. Let's stroll toward the marquee, shall we? Look, just over there, you see the man talking to the naval officer? That's James Callaghan, the MP. He was in the navy himself during the war. And there's the Archbishop of Canterbury having a word with the Director General of the BBC. Would you like me to introduce you?"

"Oh, my dear Mr. Harlow, I couldn't possibly impose

myself on such distinguished personages! I am a simple retired schoolteacher, a person of no consequence whatever. I should have no idea what to say to the Archbishop. In spite of his being in a sense a local resident. Canterbury is quite near to Plummergen, you see . . . but I was forgetting, the Archbishop doesn't live there, of course, does he? No, no, it is more than enough—a great delight indeed— to be able to look forward to mentioning to the vicar and Miss Treeves that I found myself so close to His Grace."

"Very well, then, but I must find you somebody you would enjoy talking to, Miss Seeton. Tell me, what did you teach before you retired?"

"It is of small importance, but as a matter of fact, I taught art."

"Oh, you're an *artist*! How fascinating! I'm pretty sure the president of the Royal Academy and Lady Casson are on the invitation list: I'll keep an eye out for them—"

"Oh, I couldn't *possibly*! Besides, I fear you are in error in thinking me an artist. I realized at a very early stage that the most I could hope for would be to teach, to try to help young people to appreciate art . . . and to rejoice if I were to be privileged to help and encourage one or two *real* potential artists. And now, you have been more than kind, Mr. Harlow, but I have already trespassed on your goodwill for far too long. . . ."

"Well, if you're quite sure, Miss Seeton. I expect you're ready for a cup of tea anyway. It has been a pleasure to meet you, and I may well seek you out again a little later. . . . oh, look, I think they're coming out!" There was a flurry on the terrace as the bandmaster brought a selection from *Salad Days* to an abrupt halt in mid-chorus. There followed some bellowing of orders which were incomprehensible to the great majority present; and then the strains of "God Save the Queen" drifted over the throng.

* * *

Ten minutes later Inspector Harlow stood beside the head of Special Branch, some twenty yards away from Miss Seeton. After the playing of the national anthem the members of the royal family had descended from the terrace to the great lawn, separated, and set off in different directions. Now each, attended by uniformed equerries, ladies-in-waiting, or both according to sex and status, was at the center of a fair-sized circle of people.

The Queen was completely invisible within her dense thicket. The Duke of Edinburgh's head appeared intermittently above those of his admirers; while Princess Alexandra was also tall enough to be in view from time to time; her manner impeccably courteous, her expression conveying just a hint of private amusement.

Miss Seeton had attached herself to none of these entourages, but was standing just outside one of the marquees in which refreshments were being served, a cup of tea in one white-gloved hand and a serene look on her face.

Fenn was in a good humor. "Well, you got a make on her early enough, Harlow. What on earth were you doing, though? You looked for a moment as if you were about to expose yourself."

"Quite the reverse, I assure you, sir. To tell the truth, the famous battling brolly very nearly ruined my social life. She got me with the ferrule, right in the——"

"Rather suspected something like that. Everything under control otherwise?"

"Yes, sir. At least it gave me an excuse for introducing myself and confirming I had the right person. Also got her to mention she used to teach art. Hardly a close professional connection with the subject, but it'll have to do as a reason for me to introduce them. So as soon as I can find the subject, I'll take him over to her."

"No need to keep calling him 'the subject,' Harlow. Makes you sound like one of those sleazy inquiry agents who bang on the doors of hotel rooms by arrangement and then give evidence in divorce cases. Man's name's Tump, Wormelow Tump, and an extraordinarily silly name it is."

"Yes, sir. He's definitely here somewhere; I've checked. I just hope to goodness he's not somewhere in the middle of that mob round HM."

"Shouldn't think so. Hardly HM's cup of tea, I'd say. Got on famously with old Queen Mary until she died, though. She used to make Tump go trailing round antiques shops with her, I'm told. Wonder if it's true she was inclined to forget to pay, accidentally on purpose? Anyway, what do you make of her? Miss Seeton, not Queen Mary."

Harlow shrugged. "Apart from being a menace with that umbrella, rather an old sweetie, I thought. Mild, inoffensive, *Daily Telegraph*–reading, patriotic . . . look at the way she's drinking all this in, sir. Biggest day in her life, I should think."

"Don't underestimate her. She's not attempting to get near any of the royals. She's just watching the other people watching them. And we're watching her watching them watching them. And I personally wouldn't even attempt to guess what's going through her mind. Oh, I nearly forgot to mention the most important thing you need to know: She's recently met Wormelow Tump."

"Ah. That *is* useful to know."

"Only casually, I understand, at some sort of private view. But it does mean they're not complete strangers to each other. Look, isn't that Tump over there, stuffing cucumber sandwiches and talking to that limp-looking fellow with the droopy mustache?"

Harlow peered in the direction indicated. "Where? Oh, yes, now I see him. That's him, sir."

"Who's the chap he's with?"

"Not sure, sir, but I have a vague idea he has something to do with one of the museums or big art galleries."

"All to the good if he has. Well, take the good lady over to them, Inspector, keep the conversation going as long as you decently can, and remember, I want as near to a verbatim account as you can manage."

At teatime Mel Forby was still puzzled, but not so much as she had been before lunch. Then, while passing through the lobby of the White Swan with the intention of going out for a walk, she had seen a well-dressed, good-looking man arrive and been near enough to the desk to observe him charming the receptionist. Having a vague idea she'd seen him before somewhere, she approached the desk herself and began to leaf through the brochures on display. When the newly arrived guest had disappeared up the splendid staircase, key and overnight bag in hand, she caught the receptionist's eye and the two women exchanged a conspiratorial smile.

"Dishy," Mel said to her.

"He certainly is. I bet you don't know who he is, though. He's a famous gossip columnist." The young woman sighed. "Must know any amount of really glamorous women."

After hearing the name of the paper and being told the name the man had written in the register, Mel had made a few more casual remarks and then gone out for her walk. She needed to think, for she knew the columnist in question personally, and he certainly wasn't the man who had walked in the door of the hotel. That man was an impostor.

Now, three or four hours and a few telephone calls later, she knew for sure where she had seen him before. At the Club Mondial. She also knew who he was, and quite a lot about him. What she was still trying to work out was why he should be staying at the White Swan in Canterbury under an assumed name.

Mel finished her piece of cake and sipped some tea. It

was an intriguing little mystery, and one worth looking into. There might well be a story in it for her. Meantime, mustn't forget that Miss Seeton was at Buckingham Palace, enjoying a taste of high life. Wonder how she's getting on among all the nobs?

chapter
~14~

"I'M AFRAID I've lost her, sir. Well, not exactly, She's inside the Palace somewhere, with Wormelow Tump. But I couldn't follow without alerting him."

"Doesn't matter in the least. In fact, I'm very pleased to hear it. I realize you've been left very much in the dark over what all this is about, Inspector, but take my word for it, you've done a good job. You were told to engineer a meeting between Miss Seeton and Wormelow Tump: you did so."

"But you wanted an account of their conversation."

"Well, yes, I know I did say that, but that was when I was taking it for granted they'd just chat for a minute or two and then go their separate ways. What did they talk about while you *were* with them?"

Inspector Harlow put his empty teacup and saucer down on a convenient table, delicately licked a spot of cream from one finger, and then turned to his superior with a sigh. "With the best will in the world, sir, I'm afraid I couldn't possibly do it verbatim. Miss Seeton has the weirdest conversational style I've ever come across. It's not so much that she's woolly-minded, just that she chases every random idea that floats into her head and then keeps going back and correcting herself. A psychologist taking her through a word association test would be in seventh heaven."

"I take your point. I've heard her in action myself. Just give me the gist."

"Right, sir. I should explain first that when I introduced myself to Miss Seeton, I spun her a yarn about being in the press and PR office here, and I'm sure she swallowed it whole. I didn't quite know the best line to take with Tump, though. I know him by sight well enough, of course; seen him around from time to time but never spoken to him."

"I know. That's why I picked you for this job."

"Yes, I realize that, sir. But he comes here at least once a week, sometimes more often, so I can't of course be sure he hasn't noticed me, and conceivably put two and two together. When I took Miss Seeton over to him—the other chap had peeled off by then—he looked at me in a quizzical sort of way, but it could easily just have been that he had a notion he'd seen me before and was wondering where. So I decided to play safe and tell him more or less the same thing I'd told her, in case she referred to it. I'll go and have a word with the press secretary soon and square it with him."

"Yes, yes, we pay you to use your head. Get on with it."

"Sorry, sir. Well, Tump remembered meeting Miss Seeton at the gallery in Bond Street all right, and they started gassing away like old friends. She thanked him for helping somebody called Miss Lazenby, I think it was—"

"Naseby, actually. Go on."

"Ah. Anyway, this Miss Naseby seems to have had some trouble involving her uncle and the local vicar. Miss

Seeton went on about it at some length, but I couldn't really grasp what it was all about, except that she's fine now. Miss Naseby, that is." Harlow paused in some confusion, and apologized. "Sorry, sir. Her way of talking seems to be infectious. After finally finishing with Miss Naseby they got on to the subject of Cedric Benbow. You know, sir, the upmarket fashion photographer."

"I know. He's currently in Kent, taking pictures for *Mode* magazine at a country house near Miss Seeton's village."

"Ah. Rytham Hall would that be?"

Fenn nodded, and Harlow looked pleased.

"Well, that clears a bit of the fog in my mind at least. It seems this chap Benbow is a personal friend of both Tump and Miss Seeton. She was at art school with him, apparently. Don't know where Tump met him, but Benbow's invited him to go down to this Rytham Hall place tomorrow to watch him at work. Miss Seeton was saying she'd look forward to seeing him again there. By this time the pair of them were more or less ignoring me, which was fine. Then there was some conventional chat of the do-you-come-here-often? kind, and Tump swanked a bit about having an apartment and a proper office in St. James's Palace up the road, and what he called a cubbyhole here near the vaults where some of the stuff is kept. Gifts from overseas bigwigs that have to be fetched out when the relevant ambassador or whatever comes to lunch, I suppose."

"Have you ever seen it, Harlow? This cubbyhole of his?"

"'Fraid not, sir. I've been assigned here for nearly a year, but I doubt if I've been in a quarter of the rooms in this rabbit warren of a place as yet. Well, as you might imagine, when he offered to show it to her, Miss Seeton was all agog, and Tump towed her away toward the terrace, rather obviously excluding me from the invitation.

My guess is that Miss Seeton is being shown some of the more interesting bits and pieces in Tump's glory hole at this very moment."

"I must say, Miss Seeton, I have very seldom enjoyed showing a visitor round this room as much as I have today, and oh, good heavens, I'd quite forgotten about that!" The austere, loftily poised Sir Wormelow Tump had in the space of half an hour turned into a gangling, overgrown schoolboy uttering badly suppressed whoops of glee, chortling, and pulling silly faces as he produced one grotesque trophy after another for Miss Seeton's inspection. She, needless to say, was too much of a lady to *say* anything impolite, but there was a twinkle in her eyes that a few of those who knew her best would have recognized as betraying the fact that she was having a wonderful time.

Miss Seeton gazed around her delightedly. What *fun* it was all turning out to be! Quite apart from being brought *into* the actual building itself past several footmen, one of whom had clearly been on the very *point* of objecting to her presence until Sir Wormelow spoke to him rather severely and showed him a plastic-covered card of some kind he took from an inside pocket.

Naturally one would have rather liked to linger for a few moments in the lofty, richly furnished ground-floor rooms, but it would have been most impolite to have hinted as much. Besides, many distinguished visitors were no doubt admitted to those areas during the course of an average year; but how many of them were beckoned through a green baize door and guided through service corridors and down uncarpeted stairs into a basement labyrinth? Past mysterious locked doors behind which one could so easily imagine Aladdin's caves filled with rare treasures of gold, silver, lacquer, ebony, ivory, amber, cloisonné, inlays of rare woods, exquisitely worked jewelry and oh, the list was probably endless, and all entrusted to Sir Wormelow's expert care!

Disappointing as it was, of course one had quite understood that it was out of the question to go into any of those vaults, whose doors resembled those of huge safes and which could not, Sir Wormelow had explained, be opened save by *two* responsible officials together. But how exciting anyway to see the custodian's own "cubbyhole": in fact, a small but delightful study crammed with things one would have thought of as treasures in their own right. And now the most diverting treat of all, the so-called "Chamber of Horrors"—how very droll of His Royal Highness to have thought of such an apt name for this huge room lined with shelves crammed with the most extraordinary objects and constructions!

"What do you make of this, then?" Tump inquired, descending from his small stepladder, an object resembling a small coconut in his hand. "Now, that alleged abominable snowman's head one of the sherpas in Nepal gave them—the one I showed you earlier—was completely bogus, of course, but this is the real thing. Genuine shrunken human head. Edward the Seventh seems to have acquired it some time around around 1890, while he was Prince of Wales. He had it mounted as a paperweight, but it seems Queen Victoria was not amused, so it was shunted down here. My predecessor kept it on the desk. He thought himself something of a wag—paralyzing old bore, actually—and used to like to say 'I have a very hard head, you know; it's on my desk.' Frankly I thought that was rather *too* much, so I put it in here. I did lend it out once a few years ago, as a matter of fact. To a boy called Greatorex, lad who lived in the Mews; father a chauffeur I fancy. Douglas Greatorex, that was his name."

Miss Seeton took the grisly thing into her hands without a qualm and studied it with interest. "Good gracious," she

said in an absentminded sort of way, for something about
the censorious expression on the leathery little face put her
in mind of Mr. Gladstone in the famous photograph. By
Julia somebody. "Whatever did he want it for?"

"To take to school. Not far from here, St. Peter's Pri-
mary in Lower Belgrave Street. A lot of the youngsters
who live in the Royal Mews go there. He put it on the
nature table, I believe. His teacher had been getting bored
with catkins and pussy willows, and starfish from South-
end, and appealed to the children to show a bit of imagination. Everyone thought it a jolly good wheeze, Douglas
told me, and he was the toast of the school for a few days,
but then a visiting lady inspector from the education office
saw it and got frightfully ratty for some reason. Upshot
was that the teacher was on the carpet for corruption of
youth—"

"Just like Socrates," Miss Seeton murmured, nodding
gently.

"Who? Oh, Socrates. Yes, very similar situation when
you think about it, except that I gather this chap was let
off. Headmaster thought a lot of him and never could stand
that particular inspector anyway. All the same, young
Greatorex was told he'd better return it whence it came."

Wonky Tump looked at his wristwatch, his happy little
smile faded, and the senior establishment figure who was
Sir Wormelow returned to claim his place. "Time flies, I'm
afraid, Miss Seeton, duty calls, and all that sort of thing.
I'd love to show you the stuffed unicorn some old fraud
gave to Queen Victoria and one or two other things, but we
really ought to be. . . . I'll lead the way, shall I?" He made
at once for the open door and had disappeared through it
before Miss Seeton quite realized what was happening.
The sound of his voice floated back into the room. "Just
pull the door to behind you; it'll lock itself. All that ghastly
rubbish hardly rates top security treatment." She hastened

to follow, and the moment after she had closed the door as instructed, realized she was still holding the shrunken head. Appalled, she set off in pursuit of Sir Wormelow, who was still forging ahead down the corridor with his back to her, and still talking. "Now, since you've come all this way, if HM hasn't gone in yet, I really ought to present you . . ."

"No, no, Sir Wormelow, you have already been much too kind, and in any case I simply couldn't, and oh, dear, I don't quite know how to explain this, but . . ." Miss Seeton's feeble protests echoed behind the custodian of the Royal Collection of Objets de Vertu as she trailed behind him; but he paid no attention to her and pressed on. Distractedly, Miss Seeton did her best to keep up with him, pausing only long enough to pop the head into her fortunately capacious handbag. It was as well she did so before Sir Wormelow led the way back through the green baize door and, confused and out of breath, Miss Seeton found herself once more passing through the splendid staterooms.

For, having offered her hand to dozens of gentlemen in morning suits or military uniforms of every gaudy hue, acknowledged the curtsies of as many ladies, exchanged a few words with the ambassadors and high commissioners led forward by her equerries and had one really interesting conversation, with the little man who would probably end the season as champion jockey, Her Majesty had in fact decided to withdraw and put her feet up in her private apartments. Escorted now only by a single lady-in-waiting and one equerry in RAF uniform, she entered one of the reception rooms just in time to meet Miss Seeton and Sir Wormelow Tump coming in the other direction.

Sir Wormelow must have been taken aback, but his manner was as imperturbable as it was correct. He stepped elegantly to one side and bowed low, contriving at the same time to edge Miss Seeton out of the royal path.

Bright pink, Miss Seeton dropped a curtsy. There was no time to think, so no time to make a mess of it. The result was that it was a corker of a curtsy, worthy of Dame Margot Fonteyn herself.

"Good afternoon, Sir Wormelow." Was there the slightest hint of puzzlement in the level gaze directed first at the courtier and then at Miss Seeton?

"Good afternoon, Your Majesty. May I have the honor to present Miss Emily Seeton?"

"Miss Seeton. I hope you are enjoying yourself."

Oh, *dear*! What was it Lady Colveden had told her to say? Of course. "Yes, ma'am. Delightful weather indeed," Miss Seeton babbled, and the Queen inclined her head graciously before passing on.

Sir George had been slightly tetchy with her at first when Miss Seeton eventually found and joined the Colvedens again; but he had been happily reminiscing with another retired general over tea and she was soon forgiven for her lengthy disappearance. Lady Colveden saw nothing to forgive in the first place.

"The important thing is that you should have enjoyed yourself, my dear," she said as they strolled out of the Palace grounds and made for the main gates opposite the Victoria memorial statue where their driver was to pick them up at four-forty precisely. "So I do hope you have."

Miss Seeton was demure. "Oh, yes, very much."

"Meet any interesting people? The Duke of Edinburgh stopped and spoke to George for a moment."

Sir George preened. "Clear-sighted chap, the Duke. For a naval man. Talks more sense about what's wrong with the country than all those fatheads in Parliament put together."

"Oh, yes. A charming gentleman called Mr. Harlow pointed out a number of distinguished people to me, the

Archbishop of Canterbury and the head of the BBC, for example. And offered to introduce me, but I explained that I shouldn't dream of imposing myself on such grand people."

"Well, who *did* you talk to, then, apart from this Harlow? We looked all over the place, couldn't see hide nor hair of you."

Miss Seeton took a deep breath. "Well, Sir George, for most of the time, to Sir Wormelow Tump."

"Sir *What*? Sounds like a disease of turnips."

"Don't be rude, George."

"Sir Wormelow Tump," Miss Seeton continued equably, "is the custodian of the Royal Collection of Objets de Vertu."

"Antiques, George," Lady Coveden hastily interpreted to ward off another philistine display. "Well, trinkets and things, too."

"Sir Wormelow is an expert on Lalique's work, among many other things, and an old friend of Cedric Benbow. You'll meet him yourselves tomorrow. Mr. Benbow has invited him to watch the last photography session at Rytham Hall." She paused, looking slightly embarrassed. "I'm particularly glad, because I inadvertently—"

"Invited him to the house? Has he, by Jove! Place is turning into a regular Waterloo Station. Well, Benbow's a good enough egg, so any friend of his, I suppose. I say, he'll get an even better show than he bargains for when we catch this blackmailing blighter red-handed, won't he?"

"—and I shall be able to return it to him," Miss Seeton concluded, simply to salve her own conscience, because neither of the Colvedens was paying attention.

"What on *earth* are you raving about, George? What blackmailing blighter?"

Sir George went bright red and clapped a hand over his mouth as he remembered that Sergeant Ranger had commanded everybody present in Miss Seeton's kitchen not to breathe a word of the proceedings to anybody else. "Oh, nothing, dear. Nothing at all. Sort of a—well, a surprise party, what? Last day, and all that. Oh, good, there's our car, look. Now he's not supposed to stop here really, so we mustn't hang about."

Meg Colveden had listened to far too many of her husband's incompetent attempts at dissimulation to be taken in for a moment, but she merely smiled and allowed herself to be bustled into the back of the car with Miss Seeton, Sir George democratically taking the seat beside the driver and giving him unnecessary directions to Westminster Bridge and thence to the Old Kent Road.

"Well, you must have enjoyed talking to Cedric Benbow's friend," she said when they were all settled and the car had turned into Birdcage Walk. "I hope you at least *saw* the royals as well, though."

"Oh, yes, thank you," Miss Seeton said serenely. "And I am so very grateful for your advice. We bumped into Her Majesty inside the Palace, you see, and Sir Wormelow presented me to her. I should have been at a loss for words if you had not told me beforehand what to say."

chapter
~15~

MEL FORBY was beginning to think she had entered the wrong profession. She should perhaps have become what her extensive reading of hard-boiled mysteries had taught her to call a gumshoe. Her expression of sisterly solidarity with the receptionist had proved to be an excellent investment. Not only had it put her on the trail of Sebastian Prothero in the first place, but it had made it simplicity itself to have another seemingly casual session of girl talk with her about the handsome "gossip writer" after tea, when she was about to go off duty for the day.

Mel could not have had a more observant and informative, if unwitting, accomplice. She now knew that Prothero had gone out at lunchtime and returned a couple of hours later carrying a large bag blazoned with the name of Canterbury's most exclusive menswear shop, which suggested he had decided only on the spur of the moment to stay at the White Swan and had needed to supplement the contents of his overnight bag. She was also in possession of the much more important and distinctly disturbing information that he had consulted the receptionist about the times of buses to and from Brettenden and connections to Plummergen that evening. What's more, he'd seemed to be comparatively unfazed when told there was only one service to Brettenden, at seven P.M., and one back to Canterbury, leaving Brettenden at ten-thirty; but if he wanted to go on from there to Plummergen, it'd have to be by taxi. Unless he felt like walking about five miles each way.

Now, why should a man who had arrived at the hotel in his own car want to go to Plummergen by bus? Why should a titled front man at a glamorous nightclub want to go to Plummergen at all? Mel's telephone conversations with colleagues and other contacts in London had confirmed her suspicion that Prothero had a somewhat murky past and that he was currently rumored to do well out of various rich women. But was he simply a high-class gigolo, or did he perhaps go in for blackmailing his lady friends? In any case, who on earth could be of interest to him in Plummergen? Benbow and his entourage at Rytham Hall? The setting for the *Mode* fashion photography project was supposed to be a secret, but a man like Prothero wouldn't have the slightest difficulty in finding it out.

Whatever it might be, he was up to something fishy, that was for sure. And Mel the gumshoe planned to find out what it was. It would be simple enough to see if he went to the terminal and boarded the seven o'clock bus to Brettenden. If he did, she'd follow him in her own car. Keep him under observation the whole time. Come up with the goods on him. Whether or not Mel the private eye decided to turn over her findings to Amelita Forby the *Daily Negative*'s ace reporter would depend on what they were.

As the bus neared Brettenden, Prothero finally made up his mind to get a taxi driver to take him to Plummergen, but to walk back after the job was done. Risky, perhaps, but a round-trip of ten miles on foot was too much to contemplate, and in any case there would barely be time for it. He had to be on the ten-thirty bus back to Canterbury and well out of the way before any hue and cry might be raised. Going into Plummergen, he could easily enough kid the taxi driver into thinking he was one of Benbow's team, especially if he asked to be dropped near the George and Dragon, where most of them were staying. On the other hand anybody *leaving* the village that evening by taxi would be remembered when the fuzz started asking questions.

He sighed. Trained killer he might be, but he had never during his army career been required actually to perform in that capacity, and he wasn't relishing the business ahead. Nevertheless, master criminals couldn't afford to be squeamish, and really, looking at it one way, he'd almost be doing the old girl a favor. Some of those cases she'd been mixed up in had involved very nasty types indeed, sadistic thugs who wouldn't hesitate to rough her up really badly given half the chance once they got out of jail and who were in the meantime very likely dreaming up some peculiarly horrible ways of getting their revenge. If she had to be killed, better by far that it should be quickly, cleanly, and virtually painlessly, by an expert. It wasn't that he had the slightest intention of actually *hurting* her, after all.

Mel pulled up well short of the bus station in Brettenden and watched her man get off, look around the almost deserted street, and then go into a public telephone box and make a call. After emerging, he stood outside the phone box waiting. Impatiently, judging by the frequency with which he looked at his watch, until a few minutes later a taxi appeared and drew up beside him. It was not yet eight in the evening, and dusk was still an hour or so away, so she had no need to follow so closely as to arouse suspicion. Besides, she remembered the way to and the layout of Plummergen pretty well and wasn't very likely to lose her quarry. The old road by the canal was the shortest route and therefore presumably the one the taxi driver would take. Well done, Forby, she thought to herself as the taxi pulled away and made a U-turn. Guessed right. Waiting until the taxi had disappeared round a bend in the road, she performed the same manoeuvre in her own car almost as neatly as the taxi, and set out to follow.

Miss Seeton wasn't familiar with the expression "needing to wind down," but if she had been, that is how she would have described her mood after expressing her heartfelt thanks once more to the Colvedens when the hired car stopped outside the gate of Sweetbriars, and then waved them on their own way home.

What a day it had been! Well, ever since last night, really. One scarcely had time to assimilate any of it. Nigel arriving with that poor child in such distress: how fortunate that she had just bought a fresh tin of cocoa only last week —it wasn't a beverage one normally wanted in summer. And then the excitement of last night, the conference in her kitchen at breakfast time, the interesting conversation with the bird-watching gentleman who was so cultivated and polite but did seem to be troubled in his mind about something, the visit to the hairdresser—a rare indulgence in itself—and of course the unforgettable experiences at the Palace!

After changing into something old and comfortable and putting away what Lady Colveden had amusingly referred to as the "glad rags," Miss Seeton pottered about the cottage restlessly, wondering what to do with herself, her consciousness seething with impressions and remembered images. A little yoga practice might help to calm her down, but something more energetic seemed to be called for. A good brisk walk; that would be the thing. Yes. It wasn't even quite eight yet, it was a lovely golden evening, and she had been cooped up in the car far too long. Not, of course, that one was anything but deeply grateful to have been transported in such luxury, but that dreadful rush-hour traffic! How awful for the poor people who had to negotiate it every weekday evening!

Miss Seeton closed her front door behind her, stepped out into the lane, and set off along the canal road, so excited still that from time to time she executed a few little hops and skips.

Coming from the opposite direction in his taxi, Prothero saw her from a considerable distance, did a double take, and thought very fast. This was a pure gift from the gods. They hadn't passed a single car during the journey. His victim was offering herself up like a lamb to the slaughter in an unfrequented minor road: it was a unique opportunity. A sum of money well in excess of the fare previously agreed very quickly persuaded the driver that yes, it would be pleasant to walk the last bit on such a nice evening. By the time the taxi had disappeared on the way back to Brettenden (after a three-point turn in the narrow lane, where a five-pointer might have been better for the paintwork) and Prothero was walking toward her, Miss Seeton was still a hundred yards or so away.

"We meet yet again!" he called out in a manner intended to be genial, though an unaccountable shortness of breath made it hard to carry it off stylishly.

"Indeed we do! Good evening. I trust you have had an enjoyable day's bird-watching?"

Before Prothero could reply, Miss Seeton glanced to her left, placed a finger over lips curved in a happy smile as if enjoining silence, and then made for the canal bank, beckoning him to follow her. He shrugged, but one place was as good as another, so he followed, flexing his fingers in preparation behind the retreating little back. Come to think of it, the canal could be best of all. Weigh the body down somehow afterward, tip her in, and they might never find her.

When they reached the edge Miss Seeton turned to him and smiled again. "Mallard!" she said. "Somewhere very near here. A family of the sweetest little creatures. I've seen them several times. I'm sure you'll enjoy the sight." She leaned forward and peered first to the left then to the right as Prothero positioned himself behind her and raised his hands. It was unfortunate that some residual scruple made him close his eyes at the crucial moment, when she raised her own right hand to point, crying "There! Over there, do you see them?" Prothero lunged forward; her arm caught his; he lost his balance and toppled forward into the dank waters below.

"What did you do that for, Miss Seeton?" Mel inquired, having seen the Brettenden taxi returning minus Prothero and stepped on the gas to catch up with him. She had arrived in time to see two figures approaching the canal, but not the details of the action. Now, however, she could see Prothero floundering in the water, with Miss Seeton gazing at him in consternation but seeming to take the sudden apparition of Mel Forby entirely for granted.

"The poor man! We must help him out at once, Miss, er, that is, Mel. He'll catch his death of cold."

"Don't think he wants us to, somehow. Look, he's making for the other bank." Mel had seen the look of mingled hatred and despair Prothero had directed at Miss Seeton, and practically been able to hear him make up his mind to vamoose when she herself had appeared.

Miss Seeton cupped her hands and hallooed genteelly to the sodden Prothero as he dragged himself out of the water on the far side of the canal. "I am so sorry!" she called. "Do please come to the cottage for a cup of cocoa while we try to find you some dry clothes!"

"You know," Mel said as the object of her concern stumbled away in the general direction of Brettenden, "I don't think he trusts you."

chapter
~16~

FERENCZ SZABO left his small but delightful flat just off Wigmore Street at about eight-thirty and hailed a taxi. It was the height of the rush hour, but even so he arrived at Charing Cross Station well before nine, in time to drop in at a florist nearby and choose the perfect rosebud for his buttonhole. It was of a delicate shade of peach, which almost exactly matched that of his silk shirt and was in perfect harmony with the milky coffee of his necktie.

Ferencz seldom ventured into the country: when he did leave London, it was usually to go to Heathrow Airport to catch a plane to Italy, France, Austria, or Germany. Country-style tweeds did not feature in his wardrobe, not only for this reason but also because he had long ago ceased to wish to look British as the former Frank Taylor had, aiming instead at a tastefully Continental effect.

That day he was particularly well pleased with his ensemble. He had bought the lightweight mohair suit in Milan. To describe it as pale brown in color was to insult the artist who had dyed the material, but Ferencz thought of it as pale brown, and it was his suit, after all. His shoes had been handmade in Florence, and he looked down at them admiringly as he sauntered along the platform where the mainline train to Dover via Ashford was waiting.

Thus Ferencz Szabo failed to notice Sir Wormelow Tump, who had set out a few minutes later than he. One of the many desirable perquisites attached to his position was the use of the grace-and-favor apartment in St. James's Palace, which he had mentioned to Miss Seeton, and even at a leisurely pace it had taken him no more than ten minutes to stroll along Pall Mall to Trafalgar Square and the station.

Being a son of the upper classes, Tump seldom thought about clothes but was guided by instinct and social conditioning. Ordinarily it would have been out of the question for him to appear in Pall Mall or indeed anywhere in London in anything other than one of his far from new but well-preserved Savile Row suits or, as the occasion demanded, in morning or evening dress.

The fact that he was bound for Rytham Hall had, however, led him that morning quite without conscious thought to put on a Viyella shirt, a woolen tie, and an ancient suit of heather-mixture tweed, the sleeves reinforced with leather at the wrists. The suit had once belonged to his father, but Tump did not remember this. The points of the soft collar of his shirt curled upward, the tie was clumsily knotted, and one of his socks was inside out. In short, Sir Wormelow looked every inch the elderly English toff kitted out appropriately for a day in the country.

To his own amazement Sir Sebastian Prothero had, in spite of his ghastly experience, slept remarkably well. Perhaps the human organism could only cope with one nightmare in any given period of twenty-four hours, and his had been the long walk back to Brettenden and the ride on the bus—fortunately he had been the only passenger and the damp patch he had left on the seat had probably dried out by now. The night porter at the White Swan had been too engrossed in a TV program to notice the state he was in, and his second long hot bath that day had calmed him down.

Now, after a quick shower and a shave, and dressed perforce in the same clothes as he had worn on arrival the previous day, he looked at the soggy heap of new but now probably ruined garments he had so recently paid good money for and realized (a) that he was good and mad, (b) that he was damned if he was going to let that creature make him abandon the whole thing, and (c) that on the whole he'd probably be feeling a lot more unhappy if he had woken up to face a murderer in the shaving mirror.

In spite of everything there was no reason why his plan should fail. Maybe he'd let Miss Seeton get him down unnecessarily. Maybe she really was as naïve and innocent as she seemed, and just had a talent for getting in the way. The more he thought about it the more it seemed it *could* have been an accidental gesture that had toppled him into the canal.

Thank goodness even in his extremity he'd found the strength and determination while waiting for the bus in Brettenden to make that late evening telephone call to Marigold Naseby at the George and Dragon. He'd been in such a foul mood, it'd probably scared the pants off her. The stupid little cow had hardly said a word: just listened to his brief repetition of the appalling things that would happen to her if she let him down, and then in her flat, common little voice said yes, she would do like what he said. Chuck the stuff out of the window of the lav at eleven o'clock and then wait for ten minutes. In the light of morning he realized anew what a good idea that had been. The girl was obviously so abjectly terrified, she would follow his instructions without question. She'd probably emerge from the bathroom in the end like an automaton, and very likely as white as a sheet.

If she looked awful enough, Benbow and the others might even be taken in for a while and believe she really had been menaced at knifepoint and coerced into handing over whatever jewelry she had been wearing. Only for a while, though. The story was so preposterous—and she would no doubt recite it in such a wooden, unconvincing way—that the police would soon shake her down.

Sooner or later—sooner, probably—she'd admit she'd thrown the stuff out of the window . . . and the reason why. And what good would that do the flatfoots? Not much point in their searching the area outside the window. He'd be carrying a few twigs to sweep the earth behind him and wreck any footprints he made. Not that there'd be many: the long dry spell had left the ground as hard as concrete. And in any case, Benbow's crew milling about in the grounds for the best part of a week would have made a fine old mess around the house. Mind you, one mustn't underrate the craftiness of the forensic johnnies these days, so the cheap plimsolls he'd be wearing on his feet would be disposed of in two well-separated garage forecourt trash cans on the way to London. The sort that were emptied every day.

That would leave the police with nothing but a tale about a voice on the phone, a voice that had threatened a featherheaded dollybird with a roughing up at the hands of three goons who did not exist. They might look into the business of the photos if she blabbed about that, and grill the fellow who took them. Well, let them. No problem for master criminal Prothero there. He had located this character Harry Manning by dropping the odd oblique question into casual conversations with some of his acquaintances among the paparazzi who hung about the Club Mondial, sure. So what? Marigold Naseby and her rocketing career were typical nine-day wonder topics of conversation among them, and even if the fuzz started asking questions, none of them would remember Sebastian Prothero as showing any unusual interest or curiosity.

Manning himself he had never met, and if they were ever to encounter each other, Manning certainly wouldn't imagine for a second that the suave, upper-class front man at the Club Mondial could possibly have anything to do with the disappearance of the set of cheesecake pictures from his untidy, hopelessly insecure studio. No, whatever the girl said, the police would have to conclude that the invisible man had made off with several priceless pieces of Lalique jewelry. At the very minimum there ought to be a couple of rings, a pendant or other neckpiece, a pair of earrings, and a bracelet, maybe more. And all wrapped in plenty of toilet paper to keep them together. Phase Two, the negotiations with the insurance people, would be a real test of ingenuity as well as an excellent excuse for a very long holiday abroad; but as for the heist itself, oh, what a sweet little caper!

Sailing as he was under false colors at the hotel, Prothero paid his bill in cash, which the receptionist who had registered him the previous day accepted with a melting smile, then went out to his car. The loot from Melbury Manor was, needless to say, perfectly safe, and this fact earned the surprised and gratified attendant another tip: just ten bob this time, but still pretty handsome.

And now it was heigh-ho for the open road and to hell with Miss Seeton.

"We don't of course know where he will have spent the night," Chief Inspector Brinton said, "and we don't know where he is now, except that he certainly isn't anywhere in the grounds yet. However, he's specified eleven o'clock for the pickup, and he's going to want to be in place at least twenty minutes or so beforehand, wouldn't you say, Sir George? In other words, about forty-five minutes from now."

He sat back in his chair in the Rytham Hall library, trying hard to conceal his irritation at having had to admit the head of the household to his confidence at all. At this stage, he firmly believed, the whole thing ought to be purely a matter for the police. But unfortunately the chief constable, who thought a lot of George Colveden, had probably been right in quoting President Lyndon Johnson —in a bowdlerized form—and pointing out that on the whole it would be safer to have the old boy inside the tent, er, spitting out, than outside the tent spitting in.

"Shouldn't wonder. Won't want to hang around too long if he's got any sense."

"Right. Now, we're counting on your help, General," Brinton said cunningly, "and what I'd like to suggest is that you might be good enough to post yourself *inside* the house. On the top floor, in a room overlooking the drive and the main gates." And as far away as possible from the action, he added to himself. Might even be a good idea to turn the key on the old fool to keep him from getting underfoot.

"Don't you mean overlookin' the back? You said the feller's going to be lurkin' round there somewhere, in sight of the ground-floor ablutions."

"Precisely. And with your professional grasp of tactics, you'll recognize that if our man is the smarmy Cuthbert we take him for, he won't skulk in furtively. Remember, he has no idea we're on to him. No, he'll very likely stroll straight in through the main gates as bold as brass, counting on being taken for one of Mr. Benbow's assistants. Now, we don't want anybody to be in view, certainly not one of my men. Chummy won't be expecting—"

"Chummy? Who's he?"

"The villain, sir. In the police we refer to an unidentified criminal we're currently interested in as Chummy."

"Do you, now? Interesting. Like 'Fritz' during the war. Or your 'Johnny Gurkha' I suppose. It's a kind of dog food as well, you know; we give it to ours. Or I do, usually. It bothers them to get it from anybody else. Chummy Chunks."

"Ah. Quite so, sir." Brinton felt himself beginning to lose his grip on reality, and pressed on hurriedly. "Anyway, as I was saying, the villain won't be expecting to be challenged, and of course he mustn't be, because the whole point is to catch him redhanded; but thanks to you we shall know the moment he's arrived. And furthermore, if he *should* by any chance slip through our fingers and have the gall to try to go out the same way—"

"I shall be at my observation post with both barrels of a shotgun loaded and ready to pepper the bounder's backside. Soon settle his hash between us."

"Is it wise to let him sit upstairs with a *shotgun*, sir?" Ranger asked after Sir George had bustled off.

"No, I shouldn't think it is, but it'll keep him out of our hair for a while. Besides, you know and I know that Chummy won't be going out that way. Not on his own, at all events. He won't be going out at all, except in a squad car. Foxon's already in place in the toolshed outside with a clear view of a fifty-yard arc from the lavatory window, and you'll be off to hold his hand and wipe his nose for him in a minute." He looked at Ranger's huge bulk approvingly. "If you can't bring him down with a rugger tackle and keep him down, it can't be done. We've got a couple of chaps under cover watching the far side of the back wall, and another one with P.C. Potter in the field that overlooks the place Chummy must have hidden his car the day Miss Seeton clobbered him. There's nowhere else remotely convenient, so I expect he'll use it again. Potter'll tip us off when he turns up there."

Brinton hauled himself up out of the chair. "Come on, shift your backside. I honestly think we've got this one taped. S'long as nothing's scared him off. Sure the bit of crumpet didn't give anything away when he rang her last night? She's none too bright if you ask me."

"I've got to agree with you there, sir," Ranger said, "but after we managed to persuade her to go back to the George and Dragon yesterday I spent a long time coaching her in what to say and what not to say, and this morning she swore she'd done it word for word. I wish we could have attached a tape recorder to the phone extension in her room, but that would have meant putting far too many people in the picture. All the same, I'm not worried on her account. Even now she's still obviously so terrified of him that I'm sure he won't have suspected anything. What does bother me is that we're going to have all these extra people around this morning. I'm afraid Cedric Benbow got a bit carried away inviting all and sundry. On the other hand he does seem to have kept his lip buttoned."

"It's only three extra, isn't it? I know La Seeton's here already, but then you said she'll earn her keep because the girl's taken such a shine to her. She'll keep her up to the mark before zero hour and calm her down after it's all over."

"Yes, sir. And then there's Benbow's two VIP guests from London. Mr. Szabo the art gallery owner, and the titled gentleman."

"Sir Wormelow Tump. Crikey, what a name to go to bed with. They're due any minute. Nobody else, is there?"

"Not that I know of, sir, but that's quite enough. I just hope Benbow manages to keep them well clear of the fun and games."

"So do I—hang on a minute—" Brinton's own walkie-talkie emitted a squawking noise and he picked it up and pressed a button. "Birdlime One receiving you. . . . Don't hold it so close to your cake hole, Potter, I can't make out a word you're saying. Yes, that's a bit better, but there's no need to shout either. Down the track by the wall, you say? Just the job. No, you two stay where you are in sight of his car. Taken the registration number, have you? Good, what is it? I'll jot it down and have it checked. Right, I'll read it back . . . okay? Good, Birdlime One out."

chapter
~17~

HAVING TRAVELED in separate compartments as far as Ashford, where they had to change trains, Ferencz Szabo and Sir Wormelow Tump met on the Brettenden branch line platform. At that stage they were no more than casual acquaintances, but they conversed amicably until the local-stopping train reached Brettenden station, by which time they were getting along splendidly. Szabo in any case respected Tump's expertise, and was delighted to find himself tête-à-tête with him. He was also acutely aware that the good opinion of a man of Tump's social eminence and with his connections could do a great deal for the future prosperity of the Szabo Gallery, so he set out to charm him. Ferencz Szabo was very good at that.

Tump for his part was diverted by the dapper man with the Hungarian accent. Foreigners were a peculiar lot, of course, and in general he held that it was a useful rule of thumb to trust Bond Street dealers about as far as you could throw them. Then again, this fellow, for all his clothes, his cigarette holder, and his Penhaligon cologne,

156

was, alas, not one of us ... strange how one could always tell. Nevertheless he had a fund of amusingly scandalous gossip about people they both knew, and was able to confirm Tump's suspicions about a certain dealer in Munich. Yes, one could have been stuck with a much more tedious companion than Szabo.

In the station forecourt they found no taxi as such, but an elderly man sitting in a car that looked not a great deal younger than himself. He seemed loath to set aside the copy of *The Sporting Life* in which he had been immersed but eventually admitted that both he and his vehicle were available for hire and agreed to take the two men the five miles to Rytham Hall near Plummergen. He was almost as good as his word: the car made ominous noises from the outset but did not wheeze to a complete standstill until they were within sight of the gates. There Szabo paid its owner off over Tump's protests and they set out to walk the short distance remaining, leaving the driver peering disconsolately into the bowels of the engine.

Chief Inspector Brinton had just arrived back in the library after a final brief conference with Foxon and Ranger in the toolshed when a great bellow from upstairs shattered his relative calm.

"YOU THERE, BRINTON? Up here, at the double, man!"

Reminding himself grimly that he had himself appointed this ancient warrior as an observer, and moreover that he was a JP and the master of the house, Brinton sighed and began to mount the staircase. Sir George met him on the upstairs landing. "He's arrived! Just as you thought, strolling up the drive as though he owns the place. Chummy's a confoundedly cool customer. Done up to the nines, and brought an accomplice with him. Seedy-looking character, bit long in the tooth for a job like this, I should have thought, but he's probably an expert safe-blower or something. And they've had the gall to leave their getaway car in clear view—driver's pretending to fiddle with the engine."

Very gently, so as not to precipitate a genuine crisis, Brinton caused the double barrels of Sir George's shotgun to point somewhere other than in his own direction. "Um, perhaps it would be better to leave the gun upstairs, sir. Right, now let's go and have a look, shall we?"

Two minutes later the chief inspector gazed down from the attic window at the spectacle of Ferencz Szabo and Sir Wormelow Tump chatting animatedly as they cut across the lawn toward the part of the gardens where he knew Cedric Benbow and his entourage were currently working with Marigold Naseby. Then he turned, binoculars in hand, to Sir George Colveden.

"My word, sir, nobody's going to get past you, I can see that." Sir George nodded sternly, but looked slightly sheepish as Brinton went on. "Um, actually, though, those two men are all right. They're guests of Cedric Benbow. And that's old Mr. Baxter from Brettenden out there in the lane messing about with his car: it's probably broken down again. I expect he brought them from the station."

"Really. Ah, well. Should have remembered about them. Made a bit of a chump of myself. Heat of battle, I s'pose."

"Call it a dry run, shall we, sir? Now if you'd be good enough to keep watch again, I'll get back downstairs. Oh, one last thing—We're counting on total silence inside the house for a least ten minutes either side of zero hour. Agreed, sir?"

"Mum's the word."

So far, so good. The car was safely tucked away in that perfect spot that might have been made for it: not so carefully concealed as to make anybody who did notice it suspicious, but well out of casual sight. And there hadn't been a soul about to see him stroll casually down the track that ran at right angles to the lane, along the side of the Rytham Hall grounds, which were bounded there by a mellow old red-brick wall.

Not that it would have mattered if anybody had been about: a passerby would see in Prothero a simple rambler in casual clothes, a knapsack on his back, peaceably enjoying the Kentish countryside. Nature was collaborating wholeheartedly by arranging for a few fluffy white clouds to drift decoratively across the otherwise clear sky and for birds to twitter in the approved fashion. Man, too, was doing his bit, for a farm tractor in use somewhere not too far away laid a neighborly wash of sound over the scene, as if emphasizing its everyday normality.

The house itself was invisible from the point at which Prothero stopped, but he knew exactly where he was because the tops of the group of trees he had noted when scrutinizing the exterior of the house in his telephone-repairman guise showed above the wall.

The wall itself presented no problem to a man who had on more occasions than he cared to remember run the gauntlet of the obstacle course at Sandhurst. He had been a good bit younger then, true, but on the other hand he'd been wearing boots, carrying a rifle, and humping a large quantity of gear on his back. To be able instead to wear the light gym shoes, jeans, and a sweatshirt into which he'd changed after parking the car more than made up for the intervening years of good living. And the little knapsack that within, let's see, half an hour or so would contain the loot was feather-light on his back.

A quick look round, a conveniently placed boulder that gave him a good eight inches advantage to start with, a leap, a scramble with hands, elbows, a knee, and a foot, and Sir Sebastian Prothero was lying flat, comfortably balanced on top of the wall. His heart was thumping not so much as a result of his exertions but because that had been the first risky part, when he had simply had to trust to luck that nobody had chosen precisely that moment to wander through the trees on the other side. But fortune favors the bold, and the initial assault had been carried out according to plan. Even trickier moments lay ahead, but from now on he'd at least be able to see where he was going.

Remaining where he was for the moment, Prothero cautiously raised his head and surveyed the scene. Fantastic! The foliage of the trees gave him virtually perfect cover, but there were gaps enough for him to see the house clearly, and most of the garden on that side. In fact, things couldn't have worked out better. About fifty yards away a gaggle of people stood about, but they were all much too intent on what was going on to spare even a casual glance in his direction.

Mind you, one couldn't really blame them. Dumb popsy she undoubtedly was, but one had to admit old Benbow had chosen well in picking the Naseby piece to be his clotheshorse. And talk about pennies from heaven to compensate for the bad time yesterday evening! Benbow'd taken it into his head to work *outside* this morning, and thus give yours truly a preview of the goodies to come. Prothero had scarcely dared to hope for such a bonus. He had gone to some trouble during the planning stage to find out what he could about Lalique and the sort of people he had made jewelry for, and the impression left in his mind was very much that his pieces were intended to be appreciated inside, if not a boudoir, at least a luxuriously furnished room.

The idea of outdoor fashion photographs to him suggested a haughty young woman in a dog-tooth tweed classic suit and court shoes, one gloved hand resting lightly on

the hood of a gleaming Bentley parked outside the massive
portcullis of a Scottish castle. With a wolfhound or some
other oversize dog in attendance. Yet here was Benbow
prancing about setting the scene for an alfresco study of an
altogether different kind. He'd got Marigold Naseby
draped over a chaise longue, hardly the sort of thing normally pressed into service as garden furniture, but it looked
fine where it was.

From a distance she looked pretty good, too, in a long-
sleeve gown of what had to be heavy silk, dull gold in
color, and with a headdress like an abbreviated turban
made of the same material. This covered her ears and part
of her forehead, and held most of her hair in place, all
except the part that drifted luxuriantly over the collarbone
area. The flowing sleeves of the gown terminated in long,
closely fitting buttoned cuffs, and running down from the
simple collar, almost like that of an open shirt, was another
long line of buttons. This gave the gown something of the
look of a Catholic prelate's soutane—except that the buttons ran out above the knee so that it parted to reveal elegantly crossed, silk-sheathed legs and lustrous brown
chunky platform shoes.

Best of all from Prothero's point of view was the fact
that Marigold Naseby's waist was encircled by what looked
like a massive silver chain, while she appeared to be wearing at least three huge rings on her fingers. The headdress
was either secured or adorned at the front with an elaborate
brooch, and . . . in short, provided the stupid creature didn't
chicken out at the last moment, things were looking very
good indeed. Right, mustn't lie there gawping: time to get
going.

Prothero inched along the wall until he was hidden from
the people in the garden by a decent-size tree. Then he
lowered himself carefully to the ground, gained the cover
of the shrubbery within seconds, and crept into position

within sight of the lavatory window. There he glanced at his watch. Excellent. Ten to eleven. He was absolutely certain nobody could have spotted him.

"Bang on time, sir," Ranger murmured into his walkie-talkie. We've spotted him in the shrubbery. Better close down now until after he picks up the stuff and we nab him. Can't risk his hearing anything."

"Right. I'm at the back door now, ready to come out and join you as soon as the balloon goes up. Shutting down. Maintain radio silence. Birdlime One out."

Brinton fished in his pocket for one of the triple-strength peppermints to which he was hopelessly addicted and popped one into his mouth. It was all going like clock-work. Potter's message had come as no surprise, but it was good to have his own hunch confirmed. And now they had Chummy literally in their sights, for he had not only spotted him climbing up onto the top of the wall, but himself photographed him as he reclined there, from inside the house, using a telephoto lens.

The car had been immobilized, and its registration number phoned through to headquarters, which would probably have traced its ownership by the time he had the singular pleasure of breathing down Chummy's neck. Potter and his colleague were mounting guard over the car against the unimaginably remote possibility of Chummy's giving them the slip at Rytham Hall; and the remaining two men, with their lightweight ladder, had been moved into the track beside the wall, ready to nip over and join the fray in the garden as soon as the moment arrived.

The only civilian outside in the garden, apart from the girl herself, who had any idea what was going on was Cedric Benbow, and Brinton paused for a second, meta-phorically raising his hat to the man. Benbow might be a screaming old queen, but he could be coolly workmanlike when he chose. At five to eleven he was going to find something minutely wrong with Marigold's headdress, lean over her to fuss with it, and whether or not the girl managed to come out with her lines would pretend she had. Then, having with exaggerated tetchiness banished her to the bathroom, he would in her absence throw a temper tantrum he had personally guaranteed would keep his entourage—including Liz—rooted to their places for the following ten or fifteen minutes.

Miss Seeton was a good old soul, too, sitting there quietly in the improvised changing room waiting for the girl to come into the house and then do the necessary. With that featherheaded dolly probably in too much of a state to remember what day it was, let alone the prescribed drill, it would very likely be Miss Seeton who would help her take the jewelry off, and Miss Seeton who'd wrap it up in toilet paper and sling it out of the window for her. She might be a proper old nuisance from time to time, but she'd earned her retainer all right over the last couple of days. And to think the only reason he'd appealed to the Oracle at Scotland Yard in the first place was because he was convinced she'd somehow contrive to gum up the works merely because she happened to live within walking distance of Rytham Hall!

Ah, well, nearly over. It would have been rather nice to count on being there at the end of the day, the whole project successfully completed, Benbow's gear all packed up, and to be able to watch the Securicor van drive off with the Lalique collection intact. Still, it was quite a consolation to think that instead he'd very likely be sitting in an interview room in Ashford across from Chummy, who would by then have a name, and Brinton would be pointing out to him one by one the errors of his ways.

Chief Inspector Brinton looked at his watch for the umpteenth time and moved to a point near the kitchen door where he had an oblique view of part of the entrance hall. Right, any minute now, and . . . there she was, bang on time. Good girl! And Miss Seeton moving out to help her, reassuring murmurs . . . great!

He helped himself to another peppermint.

chapter
~18~

IN THE musty gloom of the toolshed, Detective Constable Foxon caught Detective Sergeant Ranger's eye, glanced down at his watch, and then raised his eyebrows in a silent question. Ranger nodded and then resumed his vigil at the small, high window, which he was tall enough to see out of. Foxon had to content himself with peering through a crack that had opened up between two of the wall planks. It was zero hour, and the silence was becoming oppressive.

From their vantage point the two police officers could see both the lavatory window and, since they now knew exactly where to look, Chummy, crouched in concealment in the shrubbery. The window was, like all the others in the house, of the attractive, old-fashioned sash type, the wooden frames painted white. As also in the case of the kitchen farther along, a Vent-axia extractor fan had been built into the wall alongside, but on that balmy summer morning the upper part of the window was lowered to leave an opening about six inches deep, behind which light curtains stirred in the gentle breeze.

Or was it the breeze? No! Something was happening. The window was eased down further two or three inches, the curtains parted briefly, and a clumsily wrapped package sailed out. Both policemen saw the mystery man sprint forward and immediately threw themselves into action, Ranger shouting "GO, GO, GO!" which he had noticed was the order favored by officers in command of elite special forces when storming buildings occupied by terrorists. As Birdlime Two, he wanted to give just as impressive a performance in his own way as Chief Inspector Brinton had when handling the walkie-talkie. He had prudently left the toolshed door unlatched, and Foxon was the first to reach it.

Unfortunately Ranger, crowding him from behind, failed to remember to duck his head, which came into collision with one of the four-by-two joists that supported the roof. This caused him to trip over a watering can and fall forward, his outstretched arms catching Foxon behind the knees and bringing him down with a crash. Swearing with heartfelt eloquence, Foxon extracted himself from the tangle and scrambled to his feet, just in time to see the thief scoop up the package and turn to jink back into the cover of the bushes.

At that moment Chief Inspector Brinton burst out of the kitchen door. "YOU! STOP! POLICE!" he bellowed. The man did in fact hesitate, because at the same time two other policemen came crashing through the bushes toward him. Foxon sighed with relief: it looked as if in spite of that blundering oaf Ranger's efforts they had him cornered after all. Oh, perhaps not quite yet: the crafty sod had seen just one way out of the police ambush—by darting toward the kitchen door Brinton had just emerged from, just as a *second* package came sailing out through the lavatory window. You had to hand it to the chap; he caught it with his free hand on the run like a rugger forward and disappeared into the house.

Brinton skidded round, shaking his head from side to side like a frustrated bull. "Round to the front, Foxon! Get some help on the way!" he shouted, then waved wildly at the policemen in the shrubbery. "You two—in here!"

"There seems to be a great deal of commotion in the house, dear," Miss Seeton said to Wendy, who was well aware of the fact and was cowering behind a rack of gowns in the changing room. Miss Seeton had taken her there in order to attend to the matter of the jewelry, and there Wendy had every intention of remaining for the foreseeable future. "And indeed outside, too. I think I will just go and see what is happening." Miss Seeton went to the door, paused briefly in thought, and then retrieved her umbrella, which she had deposited near the fireplace, before leaving the room.

Wendy remained where she was for a while, but then it began to sink in that for the first time in what seemed like ages she was no longer burdened by the need to follow anybody's instructions. Not the terrifying telephone man's, nor any of the confusing things Cedric Benbow and various coppers had been telling her what and what not to do. That Miss Seeton was a nice enough old girl, but she was totally gaga and you couldn't work out what she was on about most of the time, so it was a relief to see the back of her for a while. That just left old Cedric, and with all this rumpus going on he'd hardly expect her back out there in the garden yet. In any case, what with all the yelling, and the fuzz in their dirty great boots thundering up and down the corridor you couldn't hardly hear yourself think. All the same, it sounded sort of interesting, and it might be . . .

Wendy was young, healthy, and feeling very much better. Natural curiosity vied with the all-too-vivid memory of

her earlier dread. Natural curiosity soon prevailed. She
went to the door, listened, opened it the merest crack, and
then wide enough to enable her to peep out into the spa-
cious entrance hall. The scene that met her eyes was, she
decided at once, better than TV. So much so that she
opened the door wide, fetched a chair, and stood on it in
the doorway to get a better view. Even without the jewelry,
in her opulent gown and headdress she looked distinctly
Wagnerian.

Halfway down the great staircase a purple-faced Sir
George Colveden was bravely standing his ground in spite
of the fact that Sir Sebastian Prothero was posed two steps
above him, menacing him with his own shotgun. The two
toilet tissue-wrapped packages he had purloined were re-
posing a little farther up the staircase. At its foot, what
seemed like an enormous number of people were milling
about, which added to the operatic effect.

With their backs more or less to Wendy were Chief Inspector Brinton, a still slightly dazed Bob Ranger, the two
policemen he had summoned to follow him back into the
house, and Nigel Colveden with Smithers the Securicor
man, both having emerged from the music room to which
they had been banished in order to place the library at
Brinton's disposal. At stage right, so to speak, were those
who had come in through the open front door. Detective
Constable Foxon was in front, attended by a goggle-eyed
Sir Wormelow Tump and a much more composed Ferencz
Szabo. Wendy hardly knew who was what, but she certainly recognized Mel Forby well to the fore, and won-
dered where on earth she'd sprung from.

Cedric Benbow was struggling to get closer to the action, but was being restrained by his factotum and the rest
of his professional retinue, who were being treated to a
stream of ripe South London invective for their pains. Lady
Colveden, who had also been of the party in the garden,

was standing a little to one side, a hand to her mouth in horror as she gazed transfixed at her embattled husband. She almost alone among the company seemed to be bereft of speech.

For it must not be supposed that the drama of the scene lacked appropriate dialogue. On the contrary, there was an excess of it. Sir George was shouting at Prothero, who was not bothering to answer, being understandably deep in thought. Benbow, we have already noted, was shouting at his numerous assistants. And Brinton was shouting by turns at Ranger, Foxon, Sir George, and Prothero.

Then Ferencz Szabo came into his own: or, to put it more accurately, Frank Taylor did. A nostalgic gleam came into his eye, his chest swelled mightily as he sucked in a vast quantity of air, and the voice that had once been envied by no less a personage than his wartime company sergeant major roared out, effortlessly drowning all others: "BELT UP, YOU 'ORRIBLE SHOWER! OR I'LL 'AVE YER GUTS FER GARTERS!"

A stunned silence fell, into which the reincarnated Frank Taylor spoke again, this time in the crisp, authoritative tones of the regular army officer. "You there! Yes, you, the bloody fool on the stairs! What the devil do you think you're playing at? Lower that damned shotgun immediately!" All eyes, even Prothero's, were, at least for a few seconds, on the exquisitely dressed figure and the bland face from which issued such incongruous sounds. All except those of Miss Seeton, whose umbrella handle rose up delicately from within the huddle of people at the foot of the stairs, silently hooked one of the two packages behind Prothero, and pulled it through the banisters so that it fell into her hands.

"You know, I don't believe you were telling the truth when you told me you were a bird-watcher," Miss Seeton remarked in a clear voice that in its way had almost as

great an effect as Ferencz Szabo's military impersonations.
"And to think that I felt quite sorry for you when you
scratched yourself and fell into the canal!"

Prothero had whirled round at the first sound of her
voice, though keeping the shotgun aimed at Sir George. He
glanced quickly behind him and then, when it registered
with him that one of the packages had disappeared, glanced
again. Snarling wordlessly, he reached behind him for the
remaining one and caught hold of it in such a way that he
was left holding a length of toilet paper while the contents
bumped slowly down the staircase in front of him.

The sight of the shrunken head from the royal collection
and the little face gazing up at him disapprovingly quite
unmanned Prothero. The barrels of the shotgun wavered
and drooped, and with what would in most circumstances
have been a suicidal lunge Sir George was able to retrieve
his property and cradle it protectively to his chest. To make
assurance doubly sure Miss Seeton applied her umbrella
handle again, this time to Prothero's right ankle, and
brought him down neatly into Bob Ranger's welcoming
arms. Bob forced him to the floor face-downward and sat
on him.

"Got you this time, you cocky bugger," he remarked
then, laboring the point rather, since he weighed two
hundred and twenty-four pounds.

"Be careful!" Sir Wormelow yelped, leaping forward.
"That's Her Majesty's head down there!" He retrieved the
horrid curio and began to examine it with tender care, cast-
ing occasional reproachful looks at Miss Seeton in the
meantime.

Brinton felt it was high time he asserted his authority.
"May I have your attention, please, ladies and gentlemen,"
he boomed. "I am a police officer, and—"

"And a fat lot of good you were, Brinton, when it came
to the point," Sir George grumbled, advancing toward

Szabo. "No offense intended, old man, but it took this splendid chap here to divert the bounder's attention." He had at least by then broken the shotgun open, and he was carrying it comfortably in the crook of his arm. With his free hand he seized Szabo's and pumped it vigorously. "Congratulations, sir! Damn good thinking! And my sincere thanks. Mind my asking your regiment?"

Ex-sergeant (acting) Frank Taylor grinned at him before disappearing again into Ferencz Szabo. "Royal Army Service Corps, General. Leading impressionist in the concert party on Saturday nights." Then, in an impeccable rendering of Sir George's own fruity tones, "Confounded cheek, threatenin' you like that, what? Serve the blighter right if we were to take his trousers away."

The long summer afternoon had begun to soften and gild itself with the approach of evening when Bob Ranger advanced across the lawn toward where Miss Seeton was sitting in a canvas-backed chair, the charcoal flying over the surface of her sketch pad. She smiled at him in gentle welcome, but her drawing materials were tucked well away by the time he reached her.

"Well, Mr. Ranger! A busy day indeed. Won't you bring another chair and sit with me?"

"Thanks all the same, but I must be off in a minute. I just came to give you a bit of good news."

"Oh, how nice. Have you and Anne decided on a date?"

"No, not yet. To tell the truth, my mind's been on other things today. I should have thought you'd had a good bit to occupy you, too." He wagged a massive finger. "I'm ashamed of you, Miss Seeton. Appropriating an item of the Queen's property."

"Oh, scarcely *appropriate*, surely. I came into possession of it entirely inadvertently. Sir Wormelow seemed to be in such a great hurry, and I couldn't open the door again, you see. I was trying to catch him up and explain. Then it was too late, and I told myself that after all he had lent it to Douglas Greatorex, so it could hardly matter if I waited till today to return it. . . . Sir Wormelow was rather vexed for a time, I must admit, but having established that the object was undamaged—if indeed one can describe a human head subjected to such a process of preservation as being undamaged—where was I? Oh, yes. I am, I believe, forgiven."

"Yes, I should think you probably are. But what on earth possessed you to wrap it up and chuck it out of the window?"

"Oh, dear, what must you think of me, Mr. Ranger! It was a dreadful thing to do, and so thoughtless on my part. It was while I was waiting to help poor Marigold when she came into the house, you see, and wrap up the jewels for her. While I was thinking about that, it struck me that I really should wrap the head, too, before giving it back to Sir Wormelow. He had explained, you see, how upset the inspector from the London County Council had been when she saw it on the nature table at the school, so I wished to avoid embarrassing him in the presence of others when I handed it to him."

"Very tactful of you, if I may say so."

"Well, I took it out of my bag and used some of the paper to protect it, intending to find a plastic bag to put it in, hardly elegant, I fear, but in the end Sir Wormelow seemed quite happy with the Sainsbury's shopping bag Lady Colveden found for it, didn't he? But then Marigold came in, so I had to put it down and hurry to help her, you see. How very effective her ensemble was, Mr. Ranger, even though the poor child was so confused by then. And . . . oh, dear, I really have no excuse, but I became a little confused, too, and the two packages did look so very similar—"

"That you lobbed the wrong one out of the window!" Convulsed as he was with laughter, Ranger barely managed to get the words out, and Miss Seeton went quite pink with embarrassment.

"Er, yes, that is precisely what happened, I'm afraid. I realized my mistake as the package left my hand, and could think of no alternative but to throw the proper one out after it. . . ."

"You lost your head, in fact!" Ranger guffawed again, conscious of the quality of his own bon mot. "And you certainly made our villain lose his. Well done anyway, Miss Seeton. Everybody reckons you and that chap Szabo saved the day between you."

"King Edward the Seventh wanted to use it as a paperweight, you know. When he was Prince of Wales."

As so often happened, Ranger found himself floundering in Miss Seeton's complex wake. What with the London County Council, nature tables, and now King Edward the Seventh, the shrunken head seemed to have a pretty checkered history, but it would be too much like hard work to sort it out, and hardly mattered really. He stretched and stifled a yawn. "Well, in that case I'm sure Sir Wormelow's glad to have it back safe and sound. Quiet after all the fuss, isn't it?"

Miss Seeton nodded contentedly. "The Colvedens must be pleased to have the house to themselves again. Though it will take a day or two for poor Nigel to recover from his disappointment."

"Disappointment?"

"Over Marigold. He was very brave at the time, though, and that's a good omen, isn't it?"

"I'm not quite with you. He didn't imagine she was going to stay here after Benbow had finished and his crew packed everything up to go, did he?"

"Oh, no, I hardly think so, but I'm sure he had been

counting on seeing her again. But then Mr. Manning arrived to drive Marigold back to London. She had already been delighted to see Miss Forby again—"

"That reminds me, how did she find her way here?"

"Oh, she was there when the man fell into the canal. In spite of everything I do regret that, even though I now realize the young mallard would probably not have interested him in any case. So of course she—Miss Forby, that is—decided to come here today."

Ranger closed his eyes, shook his head violently, and decided to stick to one thing at a time. "You were telling me about Nigel Colveden being disappointed."

"So I was. Well, Mr. Manning arrived, and both he and Miss Forby are friends of Marigold, so it was a happy reunion for them all. Nigel was there, became very pale, and went away looking quite crushed. It was probably because Marigold and Mr. Manning greeted each other so very affectionately. Mr. Manning was very excited, and explained that he had an important new assignment for Marigold. Marigold and he suit each other admirably, in my opinion. And Miss Forby agrees, I believe."

"Who's this Mr. Manning? What assignment?"

"Mr. Manning, Mr. Harry Manning—how odd, I expect his Christian name is really Henry. I wonder if he could have been named after the cardinal?" Miss Seeton paused for a moment, shaking her head slightly. "On reflection, I doubt it. My impression is that if a Catholic at all, he may well have lapsed. . . . Anyway, he, too, is a photographer, like Cedric Benbow, but perhaps not quite so eminent. Mr. Manning 'discovered,' is that the word? Discovered Marigold. And now he is to be paid a great deal of money—and she, too, of course—to take Marigold's photograph. For a calendar. Something to do with motor tires. Pirelli? But that is another cardinal, surely . . .

poor Aubrey Beardsley, such a talent, and to die so young!"

"She's going to pose for a Pirelli calendar?"

"I gather so, yes."

"Ah. I can see Nigel would have been upset to hear that." Bob cleared his throat. "Anyway, that's her business. I've been talking to Mr. Delphick on the phone, Miss Seeton. He sends his congratulations and best wishes. And Mr. Brinton's been on the line from Ashford."

Miss Seeton's face fell. "I know he behaved very badly, but I can't help feeling sorry for the bird-watcher in a way. The supposed bird-watcher, I mean. One against so many at the end."

"I shouldn't spare too much sympathy for him if I were you. It turns out he's a thoroughly bad lot, in spite of having had every advantage. You'll be surprised to hear he's a baronet, Sir Sebastian Prothero. And used to be a Guards officer until he was kicked out for behavior unbecoming an officer and a gentleman. Since then he's lived by his wits, pretty successfully up till now. Plus burglary on the side."

"Oh, dear. What will happen to him?"

"Not nearly as much as he deserves, in my opinion. Now that he knows Prothero used to be in the Guards, Sir George won't hear of his being charged with assault with a deadly weapon. Says it's the sort of thing any military man might do in the heat of the moment."

"Well, one would have to agree it's the sort of thing Sir George himself might well do. And of course he didn't *actually* steal the jewelry, did he? I mean, it never left the house."

"Oh, yes, he did, Miss Seeton. The law's very clear on that point. It might only have been in his possession for a few minutes, but he stole that jewelry all right, and you recovered it. That's why I've got good news for you. Mr. Brinton has already notified the insurers and Securicor, and says to tell you they'll be getting in touch with you about your reward."

"Another whisky, Wonky?"

"Why, thank you, George, I believe I will." Sir George Colveden heaved himself to his feet and made for the sideboard, where he turned and beamed at his new friends. Jolly good chaps to have had rallying round in a sticky situation, and absolutely right and proper that they should have got on to first-name terms right away after all they'd been through. Take old Cedric there, for one—he might be a fairy, but his heart was in the right place. No doubt about that, by Jove. If it came to that, might be wise not to turn one's back on this chap Tump, either. Close friend of Cedric's, after all. No doubt why they called him Wonky, but who cared? Thoroughly good egg, all the same, and Brinton had been delighted with his contribution. "Your glass looks healthy enough, Cedric, but what about you, Frank?"

"Don't mind if I do, George."

"Coming up, old boy." It really was extraordinary. When you looked at him, you could believe he was a foreigner with an unpronounceable name, but when he cared to, he could sound as British as the flag! Versatile, too; feller could take anybody off. Except oneself, whatever Meg thought. She must have been wrong about that.

"Everybody fixed up? Right. I say, Wonky, amazin' how you knew exactly where the stuff the police found in Prothero's car came from."

"Not really. I'd hardly be worth my job if I hadn't been able to recognize those miniatures, and the ormolu clock, for that matter. This Prothero fellow has an eye for quality. Upset you, hasn't it, George? Finding out he used to be a regular officer."

"Must admit it has rather, yes. Guards, what's more. Damn poor show. Had that look about him, as Frank no-

ticed before he did his parade ground act. The training
tells, you know. Stayed with him; sound of a regimental
sergeant-major's voice froze him in his tracks. Don't mind
admitting it did the same to me, if it comes to that. Anybody who's ever been in the army'd react that way. What
do the head-shrinkers call it? Conditioned reflex? Anyway,
I s'pose he'll have to go to prison. . . . Pity it'd be against
the rules for me to be on the bench when he comes up . . .
but I might have a word with my fellow JPs. Suggest they
needn't hammer him all that hard."

"Don't get sentimental, George. Chap's a cad and a
crook, even if he is a baronet." Sir Wormelow's tone was
slightly rueful, that of a mere knight talking to one heredi-
tary baronet about another.

"Oh, absolutely, but you've got to admit he has a touch
of style about him. Hang it all; they'd never have commis-
sioned him into the Guards to start with if he hadn't. I was
thinking after they let him out, I might try and fix him up
with the sort of job that would suit his talents. The secretary of my golf club's due to retire in a year or so . . ."

chapter
~19~

"WELL, THERE you are, Roland," Sir Hubert Everleigh
said. "Hardly the sort of evidence you could put on a file,
and still a bit ambiguous. Assuming you trust Miss Seeton's instinctive judgment."

"Having watched her in action at Buckingham Palace
last week, I most certainly do." Deputy Assistant Commissioner Fenn glanced again at the muddle of sheets of car-
tridge paper strewn about the large table at which he was
sitting with the Assistant Commissioner and Chief Superintendent Delphick. "Sorry we had to keep you in the dark
till now, Delphick."

"So am I, but mainly because I would have enjoyed
seeing her do her stuff there as well," Delphick said. "According to Sergeant Ranger, she must have had that confounded head in her bag when she was presented to the
Queen. Mind you, I wish even more that I could have been
at Rytham Hall last Thursday. It must have been a remarkable fracas."

Sir Hubert nodded. "What *did* happen, exactly?"

"I'm not sure we shall ever know exactly, sir. The best brief account may well be Amelita Forby's exclusive in the *Daily Negative*. I've spoken at length on the phone to Chief Inspector Brinton of the Kent Constabulary and of course quizzed my chap Ranger. They're both perfectly forthcoming about the general pattern of events, and their accounts tally, as one would expect. On the other hand I get the impression neither of them is particularly anxious for the full details of his own participation in the action to be put on record. In view of Miss Seeton's involvement, it's perhaps hardly surprising if things didn't go altogether according to plan. It's not clear to me, for example, how it was that having set up a perfect ambush, Ranger and three, maybe four other men didn't manage to nab this fellow Prothero *outside* the house. Or, for that matter, how George Colveden came to be waving a loaded shotgun about *inside*."

"Still, they got him in the end, didn't they?"

"Yes, thanks largely it seems to this extraordinary Hungarian and Miss Seeton."

"Hungarian? What Hungarian?" Fenn leaned forward, his Special Branch antennae aquiver. "What was he doing outside the permitted radius?"

Delphick looked at him blankly for a moment, until the penny dropped and he chuckled. "Oh, he's not a diplomat, sir. In fact he isn't technically a Hungarian either, been naturalized British under the name of Frank Taylor for donkey's years. Original name Ferencz Szabo, which he now uses again for professional purposes. Runs a gallery in Bond Street. Cedric Benbow had invited him down to Rytham Hall along with Wormelow Tump."

"Friend of Tump's, is he?"

"Now, now, Roland, don't get overexcited," Sir Hubert put in. "I can see the way your mind's working, but just because the chap was born in Hungary, it doesn't make him a spy."

"Not a friend so far as I know," Delphick continued. "No more than a professional acquaintance. According to Brinton, they just happened to meet on the train and shared a taxi from Brettenden to Rytham Hall. They might well become friends, I suppose. Apparently Sir George enjoyed his adventure so much he's decided to establish a sort of old comrades dining club consisting of himself, Cedric Benbow—who'd been staying at the Hall and become something of a crony of his, this chap Taylor or Szabo, and Wormelow Tump. Taylor emerged as the hero of the hour, by guessing Prothero was a former military man and shouting some sort of parade ground order at him. Confused him, and gained valuable time. This greatly impressed Sir George, who reckons Taylor might well have saved his life."

Fenn was still suspicious. "And why, pray, should Colveden wish to include Wormelow Tump in this elite company?"

"Oh, that's easy enough to explain, sir. After Prothero had been arrested and Brinton had taken him off to Ashford, Ranger was left in charge and he told me what happened. Benbow went back to work in the garden. It was their last day and he had to get a few more photographs in the bag before shutting up shop. That left Sir George twiddling his thumbs rather after all the excitement, and when he found out that Ranger was going to have a look at Prothero's car, he persuaded his new friend Taylor and Wormelow Tump to potter over there with him in the hope of a bit more fun. And there Tump, too, impressed the general."

"How?" Sir Hubert was enjoying Delphick's narrative, and like all good listeners, knew when to encourage a storyteller and how to keep him going.

"Ranger had thought to relieve Prothero of his car keys at the time of his arrest. Just as well, because the lock on the trunk was a very expensive ultrasecure type and they might easily have had a bit of trouble getting past it. Well, in the trunk Ranger and the local constable found a kit of tools obviously intended for breaking and entry work, plus rubber gloves, change of clothes, et cetera. Enough to spell bad news for Prothero, but even more crucially, they also found a couple of miniature paintings, a valuable diamond bracelet, and a clock. Ormolu."

"I've never been quite sure what ormolu is," the assistant commissioner once more obligingly chipped in to give Delphick time to take a breath and reorganize his thoughts.

"I had to look it up myself, sir. It's a kind of decoration that used to be applied to clocks and ornaments. An alloy that looks like gold but isn't. Anyway, although Ranger had tried to persuade Sir George and the other two to keep their distance, there wasn't much hope of succeeding. Wormelow Tump took one look at the clock and another at the miniatures and said at once that they'd come from a house called Melbury Manor, property of old Carfax. You know, the property developer and self-styled connoisseur with the string of ex-wives. It took a day or two to track down Carfax and get confirmation, but thanks to Tump's expertise, Brinton was able to make an open-and-shut case against Prothero for that job, too."

Everleigh grinned wickedly at Fenn. "Right, well, there you are. The police—the *proper* police, be it noted, Mr. Fenn—have good reason to be grateful to Wormelow Tump. And we are now informed that General Colveden thinks a lot of him. So, it seems, does Miss Seeton. With some reservations. Her rather charming sketch of him makes that clear. She did these later that same day, am I right, Delphick?"

"So Ranger told me, sir."

The assistant commissioner shuffled through the sheets of paper. "I specially like the one of the girl. She looks a lot more cheerful than before. Naked and unashamed, you might say." Miss Seeton had again depicted Marigold Naseby undraped, and adorned this time only with a wondrously fashioned neckpiece and a number of rings and bracelets. She was looking directly out of the picture with a trusting smile, and there were no voyeurs: just a brilliant impression of Nigel Colveden disappearing into the distance in his MG, equipped with exaggeratedly large tires.

Another sheet was covered with images of Sir Sebastian Prothero, invariably in the guise of a bird, but now pathetic, broken-winged and bedraggled. "This is Taylor or Szabo, sir," Delphick said, indicating a third sheet that showed a little man in army uniform, a drill sergeant's pace stick tucked under one arm, eyes popping, his face suffused with blood and his mouth open wide. "You can almost hear him yelling, can't you?"

"We shall want it back, mind you, but this is the one you can show your spooky friends if you like, Roland." The AC indicated yet another sheet, bearing a single cartoon. It showed Sir Wormelow Tump in chain mail, mounted on a white horse. In one gauntleted hand—two fingers of which were crossed—he held a lance from the tip of which fluttered a pennant bearing the royal arms; in the other a shrunken head. "If Miss Seeton sees him as the Queen's champion that's good enough for me, and it jolly well ought to be good enough for MI5. Even if those crossed fingers mean he has got a guilty secret of some kind. Did you notice the face she gave the head? Looks for all the world like Mr. Gladstone, don't you think?"

"I think they'll take my word for it, Sir Hubert. That Tump's riding high for the time being, to say the very least. And that they might as well lay off him."

"'A verray parfit, gentil knight,'" Delphick murmured,

then observing the bafflement in the expression of his superiors, added, "Chaucer. *Canterbury Tales*. Seemed appropriate, somehow, given the Kentish setting."

The telephone rang quietly in Sir Wormelow Tump's study in the grace-and-favor apartment in St. James's Palace. It had been specially adjusted at his request to emit no more than a discreet chirrup.

"That you, Wonky? Tony here, Tony Blunt."

"Well, hell*o*! How are *you*, my dear?"

"Blossoming, but *furiously* envious. Who's a clever boy, then? A certain friend tells me you're off the hook. Wish I were."

"*Hush*, Tony!"

"I insist on knowing *exactly* how you managed it. Lunch tomorrow?"

"Lovely. Your place or mine?"

About the Author

Hampton Charles is the pseudonym of a British crime writer whose work under another name is well known in the United States and many other countries. Born an authentic London cockney, he has for a number of years preferred to live and write his books in a remote village which is even smaller than Miss Emily Seeton's Plummergen. He's an admirer of American plumbing, and wonders if the English will ever learn how to install a proper shower.